If they'd met at another time, another place . . . ?

One hand moving to her hair, Mackenzie gently pulled Neile's head back so that he could look down into her face. "Wide innocent eyes," he said softly. "Eyes of a temptress."

As he pushed her away his mouth twisted contemptuously, but whether for his own actions or hers, Neile did not know. Maybe a bit of both.

Taking a deep, shaky breath, she stared up at him, her face white. For long moments she watched him, fantasized even, because he was so very attractive, so very confident about himself. And that indefinable something that made him the man he was made her yearn for something more. What would it be like to be held by him? Kissed by him? Cherished? And oddly she didn't even need to wonder; she knew what it would be like, knew how she would feel. Her eyes prickling with tears for a dream that would in all probability never reach reality, she gave a long, unhappy sigh. If the circumstances had been different. . . .

EMMA RICHMOND says she's amiable, undomesticated and an incurable romantic. And, she adds, she has a very forbearing husband, three daughters and a dog of uncertain breed. They live in Kent. A great variety of jobs filled her earlier working years, and more recently she'd been secretary to the chairman of a group of companies. Now she devotes her entire day to writing, although she hasn't yet dispelled her family's illusions that she's reverting to the role of housekeeper and cook! Emma finds writing obsessive, time-consuming—and totally necessary to her well-being.

Books by Emma Richmond

EMMA RICHMOND

Unfair Assumptions

Harlequin Books

TORONTO • NEW YORK • LONDON
AMSTERDAM • PARIS • SYDNEY • HAMBURG
STOCKHOLM • ATHENS • TOKYO • MILAN
MADRID • WARSAW • BUDAPEST • AUCKLAND

Harlequin Presents first edition December 1992
ISBN 0-373-11516-4

Original hardcover edition published in 1991
by Mills & Boon Limited

UNFAIR ASSUMPTIONS

CHAPTER ONE

NEILE didn't even have time to ring the bell before the door was flung open to reveal her mother, her hat tilted drunkenly over one eye.

'Oh, thank goodness!' she exclaimed breathlessly as she deftly appropriated Neile's car keys and began backing down the path.

'Mother!' Neile exclaimed in bewilderment. 'Where are you going?'

'Meeting at the WI. Can't stop—oh, and if Mackenzie should come in, tell him I won't be long.'

'Who the hell's Mackenzie?'

'Lives next door. I told him you'd drive him up to Yorkshire.' Whisking herself through the gate, she turned a very deaf ear to her daughter's protestations.

'Drive him up to Yorkshire?' Neile echoed confusedly. 'Why should I drive him up to Yorkshire? It's not just up the road, you know.'

'Well, of course I know! And you're driving him because he asked!'

'For me?' she queried in astonishment. As far as she was aware she'd never clapped eyes on anyone called Mackenzie in her life.

'Of course not for you!' Ellen snorted impatiently. 'He needed a driver because he's cut his hand and I thought with your shaky finances the fee would come in handy!' Her words tumbling over each other in her haste to get away, she bent to unlock the car door. 'And don't lose your temper with him, Snow,' she warned as she climbed into the driver's seat.

'Why on earth should I lose my temper with him? I don't know him! And don't keep calling me Snow!'

'Oh, pooh! And since when has not knowing anyone

5

stopped you losing your temper?' she demanded. 'He only has to say one thing you don't agree with, compliment you on your looks, and you'll be down his throat like a dog after a ferret.'

'Don't be ridiculous!' Stamping her foot in frustration as the car door clunked to, she yelled, 'You make me sound like some sort of lunatic!'

Winding down the window, Ellen stuck her head out. 'Well, you are a lunatic—at least where men are concerned. I do wish you'd remember that a little bit of guile goes a lot further than temper.'

With a snort of laughter, Neile responded, 'It would also presumably get me exactly where I don't want to be—warming some man's bed!'

'You should be so lucky,' Ellen quipped with a wide grin, 'especially with Mackenzie. Now, *that* is one hell of a sexy man! He's also an Arien, so be careful; they're driven by Mars, you know. Oh, and darling, if you have time, be an angel and finish painting the kitchen wa—— Agh!' she suddenly exclaimed. Her eyes widening in horror, she hastily put the car in gear.

Before Neile could even frame a query, a large, dark-haired man thrust past her, a small, dark-haired boy clutched awkwardly under one arm.

'Ellen!' he roared. 'You come back here this minute!'

'I can't! I'm late.' The car engine over-revving madly, she screeched off up the road just as a black cab pulled in to the kerb.

'Damn and blast it!' he yelled furiously. Swinging round on the startled Neile, he burst out, 'That woman is the giddy limit! Where the hell's she gone?'

'I——'

'Well, never mind, it doesn't matter now, does it?' he declared irritably. 'She promised to look after Daniel. . . Good lord, are you Snow? Yes, of course you are,' he answered himself. With an abrupt change from temper to amusement, he examined her exquisite face. 'I assumed you were called Snow because you had white hair, only of course you don't.' His mouth widening in a grin, he quoted softly, 'Mirror, mirror, on the wall. . .'

'Quite,' she agreed drily as she in turn examined him. So this was Mackenzie. 'Driven by Mars. . .'

'What? Oh, hell. All right, all right,' he muttered when the taxi-driver gave a loud toot on his horn, 'I'm coming.' With an odd grimace, that might by the severest stretch of the imagination be interpreted as an apology, he thrust the squirming child into her arms, vaulted the gate and opened the cab door.

'Hey!' she yelled as she hastily followed after him. 'Where are you going?'

'To the hospital, of course!' he retorted impatiently. He hovered indecisively on the pavement, one foot already inside the cab, and an expression of baffled bewilderment crossed his strong face. 'Didn't she tell you? Oh, God, no, I can see she didn't. Look, I can't drive with this,' he explained as he waved one bandaged fist, 'so your wretched mother offered to look after Daniel while I went to get it re-dressed. Snow, I'm sorry, but there's no one else to leave him with, and you must see it would be damned awkward to take him with me.'

Well, yes, she could see that, she supposed dourly as she hoisted the now screaming bundle into a more manageable position. 'Oh, very well,' she agreed heavily. 'Only do stop calling me Snow!'

With a devilish smile that almost made Neile forget what they were discussing, he said softly, 'Well, I would if I knew what your real name was.' Giving a rakish wave, he climbed fully into the cab and closed the door.

Well, really! First her mother, now this complete stranger, who behaved as though they'd been bosom chums for years. 'And will you keep still?' she yelled at the squirming child, who was so startled that he immediately went limp. 'So I should think.' Returning her attention to his father, she was astonished to see the taxi slowly drawing away.

Oh, good grief. 'Come down for the weekend, darling,' her mother had said. Huh! 'And as for you,' she said ominously as she stared down at the tear-streaked face and the dark brown eyes that stared mutinously back, 'you start screaming again and I'll bury you in the garden!'

For answer, he grabbed a handful of her black hair and tugged it hard.

'Ouch! You little monster! You do that again and I'll pull yours!'

Retracing her steps, her dark blue eyes filled with exasperation, she grabbed her weekend bag from the step where she'd dropped it when Daniel was thrust into her arms. Why couldn't her mother be like other people's mothers? Calm, sedate—motherly! And wouldn't you just hate it if she were? With a little snort, she pushed through into the kitchen and dumped the boy in the old armchair. Staring down at him, her hands on her hips, she said sternly, 'Now, let us come to a little understanding, my friend. You can glare, sulk, indulge in a tantrum, all of which I will ignore. Touch any of the things in the cottage without asking and you will be in very deep trouble. Do you understand?' When he only continued to glare at her, she gave an unexpected smile. 'Yes, I know how you feel. I'd like to do a bit of glaring myself. At my mother, and your wretched father.'

Although he had been ra-ather attractive, she thought with a little grin—and had probably thought she was one brick short of a hodful. Driven by Mars indeed. And did that mean what she thought it meant? Curious, and not a little intrigued, she went to fetch her mother's astrology book. Walking back to the kitchen riffling the pages as she went, she read the brief description of the Aries male. Impatient, forceful, confident. Fire and ice. Interesting. Glancing down at the boy who still sat, arms folded, mutiny in every line of him, she grinned, then sang softly, 'Baby, won't you light my fire?'

His look of surprise brought forth an infectious little

chuckle. 'Don't worry about it,' she told him kindly, 'Neile is cracking up. She is most definitely cracking up!' Closing the book with a snap, she turned to survey the mess in the kitchen, and gave a moue of disgust. Newspaper was scattered in a very haphazard fashion across the red tiles, a stepladder leaned casually against the sink, and a dripping brush was balanced precariously across the top of an open paint tin.

Hey ho. Slipping off her leather jacket, she hung it behind the door. Pushing up the sleeves of her navy sweatshirt, she set the steps back in position and got to work. If I have time, she thought humorously. Time, unfortunately, was the one thing she had in abundance, and if the agency she and Thelma had set up didn't begin to make a profit soon—well, that didn't even bear thinking about. With a despondent sigh, she moved the steps and began painting the last high bit of wall.

Feeling a tug on the leg of her jeans, she looked down. Heavens, she'd forgotten all about the little boy. Giving him a warm smile, her irritation with him forgotten, she asked gently, 'You want something?'

'Me.'

'Me?' she echoed blankly. 'Oh, you want to paint?'

His firm little nod confirmed that he did. Oh, well, it might keep him out of mischief. Balancing her brush on the paint pot, she climbed down. Unhooking her mother's apron from behind the door, she tied it securely round Daniel's neck so that it enveloped him from shoulder to feet. Taking an empty ice-cream carton from the shelf, she half filled it with emulsion before handing him the spare brush. 'You paint the bottom of the wall only as far as you can reach, right? Keep to the newspaper-covered area, and try not to drip paint everywhere, especially on yourself, otherwise your father's likely to kill me.'

Expecting argument, she was surprised when he meekly walked across to the wall and began painting.

Shaking her head in amusement, she climbed back up the ladder.

Her little helper seemed to have no more desire than herself to talk and they continued silently, both concentrating on their task. When she'd finished, she rested her aching arm on the top of the steps and looked down to see how he was doing. His solemn face was totally absorbed, his tongue peeping from the corner of his mouth as he carefully outlined the skirting-board, and she smiled. He was actually doing very well.

Climbing down, she went to open the back door to get rid of the smell of paint, then froze.

'Daniel,' she called softly. When he came to stand beside her, she put a gentle hand on his shoulder to keep him still. With a finger to her lips, she pointed. 'Do you see the stag, Daniel?' Crouching down, she directed his gaze towards the magnificent animal grazing not two hundred yards away on the edge of the forest. Turning to watch the boy's face, she saw a look of wonder replace the stubborn determination. 'Isn't he lovely?'

'Oh, yes,' he breathed. 'Is he real?'

'Yes, of course. Haven't you seen one before?' she asked, surprised, then wondered why she should be; she hadn't seen wild deer very often herself.

'Only in my book. Can I touch him?' he asked eagerly as he walked forwards into the garden.

Disturbed, the stag straightened and turned his magnificent head towards them. When Neile joined Daniel, shivering a little in the autumn air, she shook her head. 'No, I don't think he would let you get that close. You have to remember they're wild. But maybe, just maybe, next spring, you might see a baby deer. They often wander close to the garden and you could touch those if the mother would let you.'

'Will it be today?' he asked hopefully.

'No, not today, I'm afraid,' she denied, rather amused that her efforts to comfort him by mentioning spring hadn't been understood.

With a look of fury on his small face, he kicked violently at a stone before storming back into the cottage.

A little perturbed by his anger, which seemed out of all proportion to the incident, she gave a helpless sigh. She wished she understood children better; she was probably handling him all wrong. Turning to follow the boy back inside, she came face to face with Daniel's father. He was leaning indolently in the kitchen doorway watching her. His light grey eyes, disconcerting eyes, were filled with an expression she didn't understand. And he was too big. Staring at him, and for some odd, silly reason feeling it was important not to be the first to look away, she examined him properly, her head tilted to one side. She hadn't really had time to notice much about him when they'd met on the path, just gaining an overall impression of his height, of dark hair, rather too long to be tidy, and a gaunt face that was absolutely fascinating. It seemed to be all planes and angles, and yet he wasn't thin, far from it. The nose was arrogant, aquiline, the mouth beautifully shaped. Trapped by her own defiance, she found herself unable to look away. Ellen hadn't said he looked like that, so devastatingly attractive, but then why should she? Anyway, he probably had a lousy personality, or no brain—and then she gave a grim, derisory smile. She was the last person who should make such assumptions on such little evidence, because they were precisely the thoughts everyone had about her. A beautiful package, no contents.

'Why are you staring at me like that?' he asked quietly.

Startled, she hastily shook her head. 'No reason; how's the hand?'

'It's fine—thank you,' he murmured with a faintly mocking smile. Tilting his head in parody of her own stance, he added *sotto voce*, 'Snow.'

Knowing it was deliberate provocation, and remembering her mother's words on the front path, she refused to rise.

'Sorry,' he apologised as amusement chased the mockery from his face. 'It's what Ellen always calls you.'

'Yes.' Beginning to feel thoroughly unnerved by his steady regard, by bright eyes that seemed to hold a wealth of experience, not all of it pleasant, she brushed past him and into the kitchen. Arrogant, that was what he was, and fully aware of his own attraction. The sort of man she disliked most. Liar, she taunted herself. He was the sort of man she didn't think she'd be able to cope with. 'My name is Neile,' she told him as she swung round to face him again. 'You're a friend of my mother?'

'Mmm. I live next door.'

'So she said, but not for long obviously—the last time I was down, an elderly couple were living there.'

'True. I've been there a couple of weeks, short-term lease.' Still staring at her, and hitching his shoulder more comfortably against the frame, he asked softly, 'Driven by Mars?'

'Ah, yes—well.' Feeling embarrassed, she looked down and began to pick flakes of paint from her nails. With a little laugh, rather amused by her own behaviour, she looked up. 'Mother's fault. She said it to me before you erupted through the front door, and—er—well, it seemed to fit. So are you?'

'Am I what?' he asked in obvious confusion. 'Driven by Mars?'

'Yes.'

'Well, it's entirely possible, I suppose,' he agreed with comic bafflement, 'if I knew what it meant.'

'Oh.' Indicating the astrology book still lying on the table, she explained, 'Mother said you were an Arien.' Beginning to feel extremely stupid in the face of his blank incomprehension, she clarified lamely, 'Born under the sign of the Ram. March the twenty-first to April the twentieth.'

'Ah. Why would she say that, do you suppose?'

'I don't know,' she mumbled. Mother, I am going to kill you, she promised silently.

His face impossibly bland, he informed her softly, 'I was born on March the twenty-eighth, if that's of any help.'

When she remained embarrassedly silent, he grinned. 'So how was Daniel?'

Relieved by the change of topic, she glanced at his son, who was once again hunched in the armchair, and gave a faint smile. 'Hostilities ceased quite early in our relationship,' she said drily. 'He's been helping me with the painting.' Returning her gaze to his father, she caught the end of his amused glance at her own paint-daubed appearance and decided that hostilities were quite likely to recommence at any moment with him.

Holding his hands out in a placatory gesture, he asked, 'So how long will you be?'

'Be?' she asked blankly. Deciding he must mean her painting, she explained lamely, 'I've finished.'

'I may have cut my hand open,' he commented with an infuriating drawl, 'but it didn't affect my eyesight. I can see that you've finished. I meant, how long will it be before we can start?'

'Start what?' she asked in bewilderment.

'Not what, when. The drive to Yorkshire?' he prompted. 'Oh, hell, don't tell me Ellen didn't explain about that either?'

'Well, yes, she did—or rather she shouted it at me as she whisked away,' she added in remembered indignation.

'And you refused. . .' he said sadly.

'No!'

'Ah, I see what it is,' he commented with sorrowful wisdom that was so patently false that she wanted to jump all over him in temper. 'Having now met me, you've changed your mind.' That little glint of laughter still in his eyes, he added outrageously, 'You don't need to worry about your virtue, you know—Ariens don't like aggressive women. . .'

'Don't be ridiculous! And I am not aggressive!' she snapped. 'And I never worry about my virtue! My confusion arises from the fact that, until I met my mother on the path, I had no idea I was driving anybody anywhere! But, having been told so, I was not told when. I assumed, obviously erroneously, that you meant tomorrow.'

'Today,' he said softly. 'Now, in fact.'

'Now? I can't go like this!' she exclaimed in horror.

'No,' he agreed as his eyes ran in silent appraisal over the paint-stained sweatshirt that left very little of her exquisite shape to the imagination. 'Half an hour, perhaps?'

Glaring at him, beginning to dislike this man who so effortlessly confused her, she gave a snort of exasperation. 'Why is it so all-fired important that we dash off to Yorkshire at this precise moment?'

'Because I have to return Daniel to his mother. Today. We're separated,' he added distantly, a definite warning not to probe.

'I see.' Staring at him, several things became clear. His need for someone to care for his son; his friendship with Ellen; and perhaps that also accounted for Daniel's odd behaviour. Glancing down at the boy, she felt compassion wash over her, then felt guilty. If she'd known that, she wouldn't have been so abrupt with him. He was probably missing his mother. Did that also account for Mackenzie's rather disruptive behaviour? Because he missed her too?

'No,' Mackenzie said softly.

'What?' she queried in confusion.

'Don't speculate.'

Feeling embarrassed again, as though caught prying, she gave an apologetic grimace. 'Sorry. All right,' she agreed, 'half an hour will be fine.'

'You are going to be paid,' he added softly.

'Good.'

With another mocking smile, he held out a hand to his son, and his expression softened as he looked down at him. When the little boy had struggled from the arm-chair, Mackenzie swung him easily up into his arms. 'Say thank you to Sn. . . Neile.'

His large brown eyes fixed unwaveringly on her own, Daniel whispered, 'Thank you.'

'You're very welcome.' Touching a gentle finger to his nose, she said, 'Thank you for helping me with the painting.'

Slowly closing the door on them, she gave a faint smile as she caught the whistled strains of 'Hey ho, hey ho, it's off to work we go. . .' And from anybody else, Neile Markham, you'd have been absolutely furious. So why not with him?

Thoughtfully bundling up the paint-stained news-papers, she took them out to the dustbin. How long did it take to drive up to Yorkshire? she wondered. And, even more important, how long did it take to drive back? Down, Neile, she warned herself—no involvement, remember? Not any more, or not for a long time to come. With a long sigh, she finished clearing up the kitchen. There wouldn't have been a problem if the person to be driven had been female. Or elderly. Her worry mostly arose because Mackenzie was young, and attractive, and very, very masculine. The sort of man it was difficult to ignore. She should have been cool, businesslike, not risen to his taunts like a silly teenager, and she wished, not for the first time, that she was able to cope more rationally with members of the opposite sex. The trouble was, they all seemed to think she was put on this earth for the sole gratification of their biological urges—although he didn't look the type to have trouble gratifying his, she thought with a naughty grin, and presumably Ellen would never have offered her services if she hadn't thought she'd be able to trust him. And he had insisted that he didn't like aggressive women. . . Not that she was aggressive, not really. It was just the continual hassle she seemed to have with men that had made her so. It wasn't really in her nature. In an ideal world, she'd like everything to be calm, well ordered, gentle. Oh, well, he'd probably sit in the back with Daniel and allow her to concentrate on her driving. She hadn't even thought to ask what car it was. Very efficient, Neile.

Hastily scribbling a note to her mother and propping it in a prominent place, she carried her bag upstairs. Quickly showering and changing into clean jeans and a denim shirt, she brushed her unruly dark hair and re-made up her face. She was just pulling on her boots when the sound of impatient tooting came from outside.

'All right, all right,' she muttered. 'I'm coming.' Impatient, had Ellen's book said?

Grabbing her leather jacket and large handbag, she stuffed some toiletries inside before hurrying downstairs and outside. Mackenzie and Daniel were standing beside a gleaming Jaguar and, forgetting her worries, her eyes widened with pleasure. 'Automatic?' she asked hopefully.

'Yes. It's a long drive,' he belatedly warned. 'Are you sure you can cope?'

With a look that told him exactly what she thought of that sexist little remark, and refusing to acknowledge that it might possibly have been prompted by concern, she almost retorted that she could drive to Russia and back if she felt like it, but then hastily reminded herself that he was a client and that she desperately needed the money. Biting her lip, she confirmed quietly, 'Yes, I can cope.'

'Good. We can stop for some lunch on the motorway; we'll probably need to fill up with petrol at the same time. OK, Daniel, in you go.'

Daniel looked extremely reluctant to go anywhere. In fact he looked as though he'd been crying again. Glancing at Mackenzie, she read the clear warning in his silvery eyes. Don't ask. With another little sigh, she climbed into the driver's seat.

Settling herself behind the wheel, she quickly glanced across the instruments to make sure she understood everything, and as soon as Mackenzie was seated turned the key. A soft purr greeted her and she grinned. A hell of a lot different from her old banger.

By concentrating on the narrow lanes that would take them to the A3, she was able to ignore the tense silence from the back seat, but once on the faster stretch of road she began to find it intrusive, robbing her of concentration. Deciding that a little light conversation might help, she asked curiously, 'How did you cut your hand?'

'Some stupid woman crashed her car into a wall. I had to smash the windscreen to get her out.'

'And do you view all women as stupid, Mr Mackenzie, or only car drivers?' she couldn't resist asking.

'What?'

'Well, if it's only car drivers, it doesn't augur too well for our trip, does it?'

'Oh, I see. No, I don't view all women drivers as stupid,' he denied flatly. 'Why? Were you about to inform me that you have an Advanced Driver's Certificate?'

'No, neither do I do much driving, or at least not for gain. Worried I might crash your car?'

'No.'

He was making it very clear that he had no desire to indulge in idle conversation, and she didn't really know why she was persisting, except that she was curious about him, curious to know why he needed to be driven. 'You could have gone on the train, you know.'

'I could. I didn't choose to. Don't worry, you'll get paid.'

'I wasn't worried,' she denied. And she wasn't; oddly enough it hadn't occurred to her that she couldn't trust him. Yet he was different now, no trace of his earlier mockery. Now he seemed morose, withdrawn. Because he was about to see his ex-wife? she wondered. Because he still loved her? She'd dearly like to know who had left whom. Mackenzie didn't look the sort of man you would leave without a great deal of provocation. . .

'Your mother said you do temporary work,' he commented with an obvious desire to change the subject.

Bringing her mind back with an effort, she gave a rueful smile for her mother's terminology. 'It's not so much that I do temporary work,' she explained, 'as try to run an agency that supplies temps for whatever work is required, be it secretarial or farm labourer. Not that we've had a request for one of those to date. In fact,' she admitted with a despondent little shrug, 'we haven't had many requests at all.'

'How long have you been going?'

'Six months.'

'Early days yet.'

'I know. We knew at the start it would be a hard struggle; it's just that the reality seems rather different from our imaginings.'

His voice was tinged with bitterness, he said flatly, 'Reality is always different.'

Thinking about her own life, her own expectations of love and marriage that had come to nought, she could only agree. 'Perhaps you're right.'

It didn't take long to reach the M25 and then on to the M1, yet she was thankful when he tersely directed her to pull into the service station. She was hungry, and thirsty, and her shoulders ached. Not altogether from the driving but from the tense atmosphere in the car. Turning to look at her companions, she sighed. They looked as though they were going to a funeral. She climbed from the car, and stretched her stiff muscles.

Sitting with Daniel in one of the restaurant booths while Mackenzie went to get them something to eat, she stared across at the unhappy little face opposite her, and on an impulse put a finger under his chin, tilting it towards her.

'Come on, buck up,' she chided gently and was horrified to see his eyes fill with tears. 'Oh, darling, don't, it's all right.'

Glancing helplessly round, she gave a sigh of relief when she saw Mackenzie threading his way towards them.

As he looked at his son, an expression of anguish crossed his face. Putting down the tray, he accused, 'What in God's name did you say to him?'

'I didn't say anything,' she denied quietly.

'You must have said something!'

'I didn't! He looked so miserable, I just told him to buck up!'

Sliding in beside his son, he put a comforting arm round his shoulders and bent his head to speak quietly to him. Feeling a bit awkward and intrusive, Neile quietly unloaded the tray. He'd brought a burger for each of them, tea for himself and Neile, and an orange squash for Daniel. Biting into her burger, she watched the two faces opposite. She'd dearly love to know why the little boy was so miserable; not that it was any of her business, but it was upsetting to see a child so unhappy.

Feeling excluded—and guilty, she had to admit, although she had no reason to—she quickly drank her tea. 'I'll wait for you at the car,' she said quietly. Receiving no answer, she got resignedly to her feet.

After paying a brief visit to the ladies', she walked disinterestedly round the complex while she brooded on the behaviour of her companions. Obviously Mackenzie wasn't about to explain what was wrong, and he certainly didn't want her sympathy. Only a chauffeur. Which was what he was paying her for. So mind your own business, Neile, and just chauffeur. Right. Buying a paper from the news-stand, she went back to the car.

When they returned, Mackenzie once again holding Daniel in his arms, she quickly folded the paper and put it on the parcel shelf. Getting out, she opened the rear door for them.

Beyond asking him whether he minded if she had the radio on, they didn't speak. She could hear Mackenzie murmuring to the boy from time to time, but was unable to make out what he was saying. Concentrating on her driving, she finally managed to shut thoughts of them out of her mind, and succeeded so well that, when he next spoke, it made her jump.

'Take the next turn-off.'

Indicating, she followed his directions. The tangle of modern roads gradually gave way to desolate wilderness, and just to depress her further it began to rain, hard, angry drops that hurled themselves suicidally at the windscreen. Turning the wipers to fast, then flicking on the side-lights as the sky darkened yet further, she slowed as she negotiated the unfamiliar roads with caution. Yorkshire looked a bleak, inhospitable sort of place.

Leaning over the seat, his eyes narrowed as he stared through the rain-lashed windscreen, he directed her left at the fork ahead, then right at a crossroads. As she negotiated the winding lane between the huddle of grey stone cottages, she stared in awe at the rolling vista before her. She'd never been to Yorkshire and, although she'd seen pictures, the reality was far different. Pictures didn't give the true feeling of space, of emptiness.

It still rained, not so heavily, but the effect of craggy hills overshadowing the small houses made her feel little and insignificant. Hard to believe it was still England, even harder to believe as she stared at the vast emptiness before her that their small island was overcrowded.

'Follow this road for about a mile; you'll see a big white house on the left.'

Nodding, she was thankful when she could pull into the driveway of the house and switch off the engine. Was this where Mackenzie had lived before the break-up of his marriage? she wondered. She didn't know him, didn't know anything about him, yet she wouldn't have said that his taste ran to this pretentious-looking villa that would have been more at home on the Riviera than the Yorkshire moors.

'Will you wait in the car?' he asked grimly. 'I won't be long.' Lifting Daniel out, he held the small body against him for a moment, before walking towards the front door.

Deciding she might as well stretch her legs, she climbed stiffly out. Standing with her back to the house, not wishing to be thought prying if someone should happen to glance from the window, she walked across to lean on the drystone wall that bounded the property and stared out over the rolling hills. Probably in summer it was nice, but in the winter it would be a very bleak place.

Catching a movement from the corner of her eyes, she turned curiously and was just in time to see a fair-haired man duck out of sight behind the garage. Someone else playing silly beggars. Shrugging, she moved back to the car. The rain had eased to a drizzle, although it was a hell of a lot colder than it had been in Sussex. Pulling her black leather jacket more warmly round her, she got thankfully back into the car just as Mackenzie emerged from the front door.

Staring at him as he strode down the path towards her, at the jaw clenched as though he was containing some powerful emotion, the bright angry eyes, she sighed. The journey home looked as though it was going to be just as fraught as the drive up.

CHAPTER TWO

INSTEAD of getting into the back of the car, as Neile had half hoped, Mackenzie climbed into the front and she edged a little nervously away from the bunched muscles in his powerful arms.

'What's with you?' he demanded crossly.

'Nothing,' she denied hastily. 'Is Daniel all right?'

'No. Let's get out of here.'

Thankful to have something to do, she reversed competently out of the driveway and began retracing their route. 'Can we stop for something to eat?' she asked quietly.

'What? Oh, yes. If you take the left fork past the village, there should be a pub.'

Should be? she wondered. Didn't he know? 'Did you not live here with your wife?' she asked curiously as she followed his directions and pulled into the car park of the Marked Fleece public house.

'No,' he denied bluntly. Barely waiting for her to pull on the handbrake, he climbed out.

With a look of exasperation, she collected her bag and hurried after him, then jumped as a voice spoke suggestively from behind her.

'Hello, gorgeous. If old sobersides don't want you, there's two here who'd be more than happy to keep you company.'

Turning, she gave the two young men a look of dislike. 'I can't conceive of anything that would depress me more,' she said icily. With a little sniff, she walked on. Mackenzie was standing in the pub doorway, a look of hard anger on his face.

'Don't let me stand in your way. . .'

'Very funny.' Annoyed out of all proportion by the stupid incident, she pushed past him and into the bar.

At least it was warm, she thought thankfully as she made her way across to the bright fire burning in the large hearth, if not exactly welcoming. There were only two others in the bar, neither of whom had even bothered to look up when they entered, and mine host behind the bar looked as though he'd like to evict them bodily.

Her back to the room, she seated herself before the fire, leaving Mackenzie to find out whether they served food.

'What will you have to drink?' he asked abruptly from beside her.

'Half a lager, please. Do they serve food?'

'The barman's making up some sandwiches. Beef do you?'

'Fine,' she agreed. She'd probably have got beef whether she liked it or not.

When Mackenzie came to throw himself moodily into the chair opposite her, she stared at him. She still felt rather hurt by his remarks in the car park. They had been stupid and unnecessary. Not worthy of him at all. And yet how could she know what he was really like? Although in an odd sort of way she felt that she did. Felt that she knew him well.

There were traces of grey in his thick dark hair, she noted, grooved lines running from his nose to the corners of his mouth, a frown mark between his well-defined brows. Mean, moody and magnificent, the line popped into her head. Hastily abandoning that train of thought, she broke the tense silence by asking quickly, 'How often do you get to see him?'

'What? Oh, once a month.'

'Well, that's not so long,' she murmured comfortingly.

'Don't be so damned patronising!' His eyes flicking up to capture hers, he bit out angrily, 'You don't know anything about it!'

'No, I don't,' she agreed, her eyes determinedly holding his. 'I was merely trying to offer some comfort.'

'Well, don't! I don't need, or want, your blasted comfort!'

'Then you won't get it,' she agreed as equably as she could.

'Good. Do you think I find it amusing to prise my son's arms away from my neck and hand him over to a woman he hates? Do you think I can just shrug it off and indulge in idle conversation?'

'I have no idea. I know nothing about you at all. Nor do I wish to if this is a sample of your usual behaviour,' she added stiltedly. 'It's not my fault you separated from your wife. Neither is it my fault that your son dislikes her.' Picking up her bag, annoyed to find that her hand was shaking, she stood up. 'I will sit over there, then you can brood on your many injustices in peace.' Her mouth set, she pushed her chair back only to be violently yanked back down by his savage grip on her arm.

'Sit down and stop being so bloody touchy!'

'Me, touchy?' she exclaimed in disbelief. 'Me? All I did was try to offer a very natural sympathy, and all the thanks I get is to have my head bitten off!'

'What did you expect? I paid for your services as a driver, not a companion, and I certainly didn't ask for your sympathy, nor your concern. Or did you expect me to entertain you? Is that what this is all about? Don't like being ignored, Miss Markham?'

'I adore being ignored,' she retorted icily, 'especially by someone like you!' Breaking off her angry glare, she turned to accept the sandwiches and drink the barman was handing her. 'Thank you,' she managed more or less politely. Hurt and bewildered by his attack, she kept her eyes on her plate.

Accepting his own plate of sandwiches and pint, he suddenly thrust one hand through his hair. 'I'm sorry,' he apologised gruffly. 'I don't find this easy.'

'No,' she agreed stiffly. Still without looking at him,

she picked up a sandwich, determined not to say anything else that might be misconstrued. In fact, she wouldn't speak at all, she decided. She hated rows and arguments, they always made her feel ill—and they could drive back to Sussex in total silence for all she cared! Glancing round her, she saw that the two men who had been there when they came in were still hunched over the bar, both silent. The barman was idly polishing glasses, his expression blank. She could just see through into the far bar and she frowned slightly as she caught a brief glimpse of a fair-haired man. He looked very much like the man she'd seen at Mackenzie's house. Before she could comment on the coincidence, or even remember that she wasn't going to talk to him, Mackenzie diverted her attention.

'You drive very well,' he complimented quietly.

'Thank you,' she responded tartly. 'Did you expect anything else?'

'From the competent tread-on-them-first-before-they-tread-on-you Neile? No, I didn't.'

Ignoring his jibe, she flinched when he put a hand on her arm.

'Hey, come on, I've said I was sorry. Don't sulk, Neile.'

'I was not sulking.'

'All right,' he agreed quietly, 'punishing me for my crass behaviour.'

'I wasn't doing that either,' she denied with equal restraint, 'and neither do I tread on people before they tread on me. You shouldn't believe everything my mother says.'

'No, parents often have a very odd idea of their offspring, deserved or not. Although I think she was trying to be complimentary.'

'Even about my arrogance?' she asked in disbelief as she remembered Ellen's words on the front path.

'Oh, well, that probably stems from being an only child. . .'

'No,' she denied, and quite suddenly, and unexpectedly, she gave him an enchanting grin, 'it stems from having a dotty mother!'

A flash of surprise in his eyes, quickly hidden, he agreed with a fervency that sounded slightly unnatural. 'Well, there I will agree with you! The woman's a lunatic! In fact it has to be some sort of miracle that you've turned out reasonably normal.'

'A compliment yet,' she quipped to hide the perturbation she'd felt at his quickly veiled expression.

With a muffled grunt, he gave her a look of dry mockery. 'If you consider that a compliment, one can only wonder at the sort of remarks that are normally thrown at you from members of the opposite sex.'

'Oh, you wouldn't believe,' she drawled softly, and her mouth twisted with distaste as she recalled some of the remarks that had been levelled at her.

'I probably would—a lot worse than the ones in the car park in any event.' With a little sigh for his own behaviour, he lightly touched his fingers to the back of her hand. 'Another apology, Neile. I was completely out of order.'

'Yes,' she agreed quietly. 'You were. I didn't ask to look like this, and I get a little sick and tired of being taken for a brainless bimbo. Despite what you, or Ellen, might think, I am not aggressive by nature; I've been forced to be that way by the sort of remarks I got today.'

'You think she doesn't know that?' he asked gently.

Shaking her head, not in denial, but in a desire to drop the subject, she looked down and picked up her drink.

'She talks about you constantly, did you know? She's very proud of her only child.'

'Yes, I know,' she agreed wryly, 'especially when you consider she didn't want me in the first place.'

'Didn't she?' he asked, surprised. 'You'd never guess from the way she talks. Did she tell you you weren't wanted?'

'Mmm.'

'And it didn't bother you?' he asked in obvious astonishment.

'No, why should it?'

'Oh, I don't know, I suppose I assumed if a child knew it wasn't wanted it would have all sorts of hang-ups, suffer traumas, be insecure.'

The way he said it, with a rather bitter twist to his mouth, made her wonder if he was thinking of his son. Hadn't he been wanted?

'Well, I suppose that would depend on the parents,' she offered cautiously, 'but the truth of the matter is that my mother's mistakes always turn out better than her plans!'

Staring at her, his eyes wide with amazement, his face suddenly crumpled with laughter, and oh, boy, what a difference that made!

'Now that I believe!' He grinned. 'I don't think I've ever met a more disorganised, scatty woman!'

'No,' she murmured absently as she tried to come to terms with the rather odd, alarming churning in her stomach. She wanted to tell him not to smile at her like that; not to display his dangerous charm, because she suddenly realised how susceptible she was to it. Gordon hadn't had charm, or anything like this man's rugged masculinity. In fact, right here and now, she found it hard to even remember what Gordon looked like! Dragging her mind back, she added faintly, 'I'm only thankful I don't take after her.'

'No. I imagine that, whatever you take on, you take on with confidence, don't you?'

Remembering the agency, and the sublime confidence she had used to persuade poor Thelma to go in with her, she grimaced.

'But then women with looks like yours aren't normally given to lack of confidence, or reticence,' he added with a rather deliberate provocation.

'Aren't they? Any more than men with yours are?'

His eyes holding hers, a mischievous gleam lit the

silver depths. 'No,' he agreed softly, 'I'm neither reticent, nor lacking in confidence.'

'No, and neither of us can help our looks; they came with the stork. And as for lack of reticence—well, I probably get that from my father. We were both inclined to shoot first and ask questions afterwards.'

'At least that way you don't get answers you don't like, do you?'

'No,' she admitted with a sigh. 'You make me sound a not very nice person.'

'Just a bit defensive, and—er—bossy?' he queried, tongue very firmly in cheek.

'Maybe. I don't mean to be, I just get impatient when things don't happen fast enough for my liking.'

'Mmm.' Leaning back in his chair, he stared somewhat moodily into the fire and she watched him curiously. What was his wife like? she wondered. What did she say about the marriage? There were always two sides to a story. . . Not that she was ever likely to hear the other side.

Finishing her drink, she replaced the glass on the cardboard mat. 'We ought to be going,' she said quietly. 'We've still a long drive ahead of us.'

'Yeah.' Straightening, he gave her a grim smile. 'It will be dark soon—do you want to get back this evening? Or would you prefer to stop overnight somewhere?'

Alarm bells jingling, she said hastily, 'We'll see how it goes, shall we?' Spending the night somewhere with Mackenzie didn't sound like a very good idea. Even if they did have separate rooms, which naturally they would, she assured herself rather too forcefully.

Thankfully, Mackenzie didn't seem to find anything amiss with her statement and she breathed a sigh of relief as he got to his feet. Telling herself she was wildly overreacting didn't help matters at all. She didn't even really know why she felt so aware of him, not on a rational level at any rate.

With a sigh for her own muddled thoughts, she led

the way back to the car, and was really rather glad when he returned to his former moodiness, or, at least, mentally withdrew from her. Not liking to intrude, or be accused again of prying into what wasn't her concern, she drove in what she thought was the direction they had taken earlier. It wasn't until they passed a rather odd-looking stone monument that she had no recollection of seeing before that she began to wonder if she was on the right road. They seemed to have been driving for ages, and surely they should have been at the motorway by now. The sky too had darkened, not only with evening but with angry purple clouds that presaged more rain.

'Mackenzie,' she murmured as she peered intently through the windscreen, 'can you see if we're on the right road? Only I don't remember any of this at all.'

Rousing himself with an obvious effort, he too stared through the windscreen. With a frown, he turned to peer back the way they'd come. 'Which way did you go at the crossroads?'

'Left—I think,' she added. In truth, she didn't really remember.

'What do you mean, you think? You must know which way you turned! You're the driver, for goodness' sake!'

'I know I'm the driver! But I don't know this area, do I? And every road looks the same to me!'

'Well, go on until you come to a signpost,' he muttered. 'Only why the hell you couldn't have asked instead of just driving on willy-nilly, I don't know!'

'Because I thought I knew where I was going! Oh, damn!' she exclaimed as there was an ominous rumble of thunder. 'That's all we need.' As if taking her words for invitation, a heavy gust of wind buffeted the car before the heavens opened to slam a steely curtain of rain across her vision.

'Pull over to the side for a minute—perhaps it'll pass.'

'Yeah, and perhaps it won't.' The way her luck was going, they'd have a flood and forked lightning to contend with next. Steering the heavy car to the side, she pulled on the brake and switched off the engine. It was like being in a carwash, and maybe with someone else it might have been cosy in the confines of the car which was being lashed by wind and rain, only it wasn't anyone else, it was a virtual stranger. A very disturbing virtual stranger. As oppressed minutes ticked past with neither of them speaking, she began to fidget nervously. Without the engine running, the interior was beginning to steam up, which for some ridiculous reason seemed to increase the tension.

Without knowing she was doing it, she began to hum under her breath.

'Do you have to make that noise?' he complained shortly.

Clamping her teeth together to prevent any sound escaping, she began to tap her fingers nervously on the armrest until he clamped his hand over hers to stop her.

Jumping in alarm, she wrenched her hand free. Glancing towards him, she saw he wore the look of a man goaded too far. Grabbing the newspaper she'd bought earlier off the shelf, she hastily opened it. It would at least serve as a shield to hide behind. Irritated by her inability to behave normally, she began to read, and when she reached the astrological predictions she automatically glanced at her own sign. 'I should have read these before I left home,' she muttered.

'You surely don't believe in that rubbish, do you?' he asked irritably.

'Only if they're good,' she quipped glibly.

'And are they?'

'No, but entirely appropriate. They say, "Librans should think twice about any journey needing to be undertaken today," and ain't that the truth? Want me to read you yours?'

'No,' he refused shortly.

Ignoring his injunction, she quickly read them through. 'Oh, my,' she exclaimed before beginning to read them out loud. '"Today's events should prove that your options for the future are not quite so cut and dried as you thought. Your life need not become dull or predictable after all. It will prove possible to experience some magic, starting from now."'

'Magic?' he asked with soft sarcasm. 'This is magic? We haven't a clue where we are. We're in the middle of the storm of the century! And, to cap it all, there's you behaving like somebody's maiden aunt. Oh, to hell with it! Turn the car round and we'll go back the way we came.'

Inordinately thankful for the instruction, she quickly put the paper away. Turning on the ignition and switching the demister to full blast, she began manoeuvring the car across the road. At least there were no drystone walls where they were, otherwise she wouldn't have been able to turn on the narrow road. Reversing and swinging it round on the opposite lock, she went back to where she judged the verge to be, then, putting it in drive, accelerated gently. When nothing happened, she pressed harder and felt the rear wheels spin. Not daring to look at Mackenzie, she put the lever back into reverse, hoping to find firmer ground.

Letting his breath out in an explosion of frustration, he knocked the lever into neutral. 'All you're doing is digging us deeper in!' He opened his door a fraction, and peered backwards. Uttering a raw expletive that was certainly descriptive if not entirely possible, he gritted, 'Give me the keys, I'll see if there's something in the boot we can use to give traction.'

Switching off the engine, she meekly handed them over. She hoped no one else came down the lane, or, if they did, that they were driving slowly, otherwise being stuck wasn't likely to be the only problem.

'Try now,' he instructed as he opened the door and handed her back the keys. 'Gently!'

Pulling a face, she switched on the engine, and, keeping a wary eye on him through the rear-view mirror as he stood behind the car, she gently depressed the accelerator. Feeling the wheels bite, she eased the car back on to the road and made sure all four wheels were securely on the hard surface before halting again. Watching him as he picked up the mat he had used and slung it into the boot, she leaned across to unlatch the door for him. It would be very unwise, she decided, to comment on his soaked state. His jeans were plastered to his legs, his heavy sweater a soggy mass that clung to him, and his hair was dripping over his face.

'I'm sorry,' she apologised quietly. When he didn't answer, she said the very thing she'd promised herself not to say. 'You ought to get out of those wet things. You'll end up with pneumonia.'

'Well, I promise not to ask you to nurse me!'

Clamping down hard on any retort she might be tempted to make, and wondering how on earth it had got fully dark without her even noticing, she flicked on the headlights. Not that they helped much, just reflected back from the needles of rain pounding on the road ahead. Keeping her speed low, she stiffened and held her breath as the car began to shudder. Oh, hell. Now what? As the previously smooth purr was replaced by hiccups, she stared in horrified fascination at the instrument panel and didn't need his violent curse to tell her what the matter was. They'd forgotten to fill up with petrol. Correction—*she'd* forgotten to fill up with petrol.

'I don't suppose there's a spare can in the boot?' she asked tentatively as they limped to a halt.

'No.'

'No, I thought it was too much to hope for.'

'Why bloody ask, then?'

'One lives in hope. What now?'

'What would you suggest?' he asked sarcastically.

'Walking?' she prompted fatalistically. 'I don't suppose you remember if we passed a garage, do you?'

'No,' he said stonily, eyes firmly to the front, face carved.

'No,' she echoed on a long sigh. 'So I guess we walk.'

'*I* will walk. There's no point in both of us getting wet.'

Which was true, only Neile didn't feel like sitting in the car on her own, for hours maybe. Wincing as he slammed his door behind him, she stared at his tall figure as he strode angrily up the centre of the road. Climbing hastily out and locking the doors, she hurried after him. Well, as chauffeurs went, she thought ironically, she'd presumably make a good plumber.

Apart from giving her a glance of surprise as she came abreast of him, he ignored her and she gave a sour smile. Not that she'd expected him to thank her, exactly. Still. Turning the collar of her jacket up, she shoved her hands into her pockets and hunched her shoulders against the wind and rain. She was soaked in seconds, her feet squelching horribly in boots not made for more than a light drizzle. Her eyes slitted, she stared round her. Nothing—no lights, no traffic, no dwellings that she could see. Goodness only knew where she had driven; it looked like the back of beyond. As they rounded a fold in the hills, she caught a flash of light from the corner of her eye. Clutching his arm to halt him, she strained into the darkness.

'Now what?' he asked impatiently.

'I thought I saw a light—yes, there!' she exclaimed, pointing.

'Probably a farm,' he muttered. Not giving her a chance to answer, he grabbed her arm and hurried her towards it.

There was nothing so dignified as a farm gate, merely a gap in the low wall and a quagmire of a path straggling towards a small stone building. One tiny window showed a rectangle of pale light. Well, it was better than nothing, she thought philosophically. At least it offered shelter. As Mackenzie strode ahead to the door, she huddled miserably beside him, shivering. Rapping on the door with his fist, he muttered impatiently under his breath until the door creaked open barely enough for someone to put their eye to the crack.

'Yes?'

Explaining quickly to the barely seen female presence, Mackenzie asked if she had a telephone they might use.

'No, dear,' then with an exclamation of impatience, as though she couldn't be doing with this hiding behind doors, she opened it fully to reveal a grey-haired woman in her seventies, Neile would have guessed, her face lined and wrinkled, her eyes kind. 'Nearest phone would be at Letty's place, but that's a good four mile down the road, not that she'd be in if you went, like. She's away in Leeds this week. Oh, look, you can't stand out there in this! Come on in, do! Look at you, soaked to the skin, the pair of you!'

The front door opened directly on to the living-room, and, politely ushering Neile in first, Mackenzie joined her by the small open grate as she held her hands out to the fitful blaze.

'Is there a garage near by?' he asked without the least vestige of hope in his voice.

'Bless you, no, dear, not round here. There's one of them service stations over at Hadwell, but that's a good seven mile away! What on earth made you come down this road?'

'We got lost,' he explained flatly.

'I got lost,' Neile corrected quietly with an expressive grimace, and the woman chuckled.

'Oh, dear. In trouble, are you?' she asked softly, and they both peeked towards Mackenzie.

To give him his due, he had the grace to look slightly ashamed of himself and the woman gave his arm a sympathetic pat. 'Well, now, least said soonest mended, I always say, and the first thing is for you to get out of them wet things. I'm Mrs Goff, by the way; I'll put the kettle on, find you something to wear and then we can put our heads together and see what's best to be done.'

'Thank you, we're very grateful,' Neile said quietly.

'Well, no doubt you'd do the same for me if I was caught in your neck of the woods. Now come on, get out of them wet clothes!' Turning she walked slowly out to what Neile presumed was the kitchen.

'Magic?' he asked softly.

Biting her lip, she peeped towards him. 'It could be worse,' she offered tentatively.

'It could?' he asked drily. 'How?'

With a little chuckle, she shrugged out of her jacket then sat down to remove her sodden boots. At least he had a sense of humour. 'Need a hand?' she asked as she watched her companion struggle to remove his own ankle boots. With only one hand operational, he was having a great deal of difficulty. Without waiting for a reply, she knelt before him and tugged them off.

'Thanks.'

Getting to her feet, she smiled as Mrs Goff returned. She was carrying two flannelette sheets, and Ncile's smile died. 'Couldn't find anything else. Will they do?' she asked worriedly.

'They'll do fine, thank you,' Mackenzie said quickly.

Nodding, she went back to the kitchen.

Automatically taking the sheet Mackenzie held out to her, Neile stared at it in horrified fascination.

'It was the best she could do,' he said quietly.

Her throat dry, she nodded. 'I'll—er—go and get changed in the kitchen——'

'Neile,' he interrupted softly, and she looked at him in alarm. 'Don't look like that,' he cautioned with a gentleness hitherto unshown. 'It will be perfectly all right, I promise. I'll turn my back, all right? All right?' he insisted when she remained mute.

Dragging a shaky breath into her lungs, she nodded and turned her own back. For God's sake, she scolded herself, you've undressed on beaches! Used communal changing-rooms in boutiques. . . But it wasn't the same. It most assuredly wasn't the same! As he very well knew.

Putting the thankfully large sheet round her shoulders

like a cape, she began to remove her clothes within the concealing folds. Suddenly becoming aware of muttered cursing behind her, she swung round, her eyes wide. He was naked to the waist and was trying to undo his wet jeans one-handed. Don't ask *me*, she prayed.

'Well, don't just stand there with your mouth open, Neile,' he exclaimed irrascibly.

'What do you expect me to do?' she asked faintly.

'What do you think I expect you to do? Knit a sweater? I need you to undo the damned zip.'

When she didn't answer—wasn't sure she could answer—he looked up, and at the expression on her face he slowly smiled. A distinctly evil smile, Neile decided.

'Please?' he taunted softly. 'You wouldn't want me to get pneumonia, now would you? Don't answer that. . .'

Taking a deep breath, she marched across, knocked his hand aside and, without allowing herself to consider that she might accidentally touch parts of him she had no wish to touch, she firmly grasped the metal tag on his jeans and gave a tug. 'There you are; manage now, can you?'

'I think so, thank you,' he said softly.

'Don't laugh! Don't you dare laugh!' she warned him, and to her absolute horror her voice came out cracked and squeaky.

Deliberately holding her eyes with his, he said with quiet solemnity, 'I'm not laughing, Neile. Believe me, I truly am not laughing.'

Feeling gauche and stupid, and far too warm, she quickly swung away, only to swing back when he gave a long, despairing sigh.

'Oh, God. I think it would be easier to catch pneumonia.' Looking up at her, a helpless expression on his strong face, he pleaded, 'Please? I can't get them off. I think they've shrunk.'

Very carefully keeping her face averted, she walked behind him and grasped his jeans at each side of the waistband and attempted to ease them down. 'They won't budge,' she said woodenly.

'Then pull harder.'

Her mouth compressed, she lay her face against his smooth naked back—a very warm, smooth naked back—took a firmer grip, and, quite irrationally terrified of taking his pants with them, she closed her eyes and yanked hard. Walking round to his front, her face still averted, she pushed him backwards on to the sofa, lifted his legs and yanked the offending material from his feet.

'Thank you.'

'Pleasure,' she muttered. Annoyed with herself for being so embarrassed, annoyed with him for causing it, she struggled out of her own jeans and shirt. Dropping them on the floor she hastily, and very thankfully, wrapped herself toga-like in the sheet.

Without a word, Mackenzie gathered up their wet clothing and took them out to the kitchen. He hadn't seemed embarrassed, and yet had more cause, and she wished fervently that she could match his insouicence.

When he returned, she glanced at him sideways, then gave a sheepish smile at his expression of controlled amusement.

'It's daft, I know.'

'Very,' he agreed.

Determined to prove that she could be sensible, she patted the sofa beside her. 'Come and get warm—you're shivering.'

'Pneumonia, do you think?' he asked blandly and she gave another smile.

'Oh, pleurisy at the very least. . .'

'With complications,' he insisted with a little nod that reminded Neile very much of his son. 'I do hate to be mundane.'

'I doubt you'd ever be accused of being that,' she murmured as she held her hands out to the fitful blaze.

'Do you, Neile?'

'Yes,' she said drily. 'So, did you and Mrs Goff come

up with a plan? A hardy steed that just happens to be in the stable that you could ride? An ancient bicycle?'

'No, not even a magic carpet. However, Brenda——'

'Brenda?' she queried comically.

'Yes, Brenda,' he repeated firmly, 'daughter number one of Mrs Goff, will be by early in the morning, as she is every morning, to check on her mother, and——'

'If we're very good, and you smile nicely at Brenda, she will give you a lift to the garage?'

'Correct.'

'Which means we spend the night here?'

'Yes. Mrs Goff couldn't possibly consider the appalling prospect of my walking seven miles to the service station and adding further complications to my pleurisy. . .'

Her lips twitching, she stared about her. It was a very small room, gloomy, by reason of the fact that there was no electricity, sparsely furnished, and, even with the fire in the grate, cold. 'How many bedrooms are there?' she asked absently. When he didn't immediately answer, she looked at him, and a little shiver of alarm raced along her nerves. Jerking her eyes from his, she stared at the fire.

'One?' she queried huskily.

'One,' he confirmed.

'Ah.'

'Quite so, and we can hardly expect Mrs Goff to relinquish her bed to us.'

'No.'

'Which leaves the sofa. . .'

Taking a deep breath and holding it in her lungs, she made a pretence of examining the inadequate length of the sofa.

'If it bothers you that much, Neile,' he said quietly, 'I'll sleep on the floor. Or try to.'

'No. Don't be silly, it'll be fine,' she lied carefully. In an effort to dispel the awful tension that was cramping her muscles, she added hastily, '"See how it goes", did I say when you asked me if I wanted to stop somewhere overnight?'

'You did.'

'Hmm. Didn't go very well, did it?'

'No, Neile, it didn't,' he said gently.

'No,' she agreed despondently. 'I'm sorry. Better not add chauffeuring to my list of abilities, then, had I?'

'Any more than I should add passenger to mine?' he queried softly, and she looked at him in surprise. She hadn't expected that—that he would apologise. 'I am sorry, Neile, I've been an absolute bastard. It's never easy taking Daniel back, especially today when we've only had a week together. But while I'm fighting for custody I have to behave, keep only to my allotted days.'

'And will she? Let you keep him, I mean?'

'For a large sum, yes,' he agreed with careful neutrality.

'And can you afford it? Sorry,' she grimaced awkwardly, 'that was impertinent. I didn't mean to be nosy.'

'Yes, I can afford it,' he agreed quietly, 'and there's no need to apologise. I brought the subject up, after all.' Leaning back, pulling the folds of the sheet across his shoulders, inadvertently exposing a long length of leg, he turned his head to look at her. 'Are you always this defensive?'

'I wasn't aware that I was——'

'Yes, you are,' he contradicted. 'You seem terrified of encroaching on anyone else's life, and even more terrified that someone will do the same to you.'

'Do I?' Turning her face away, she frowned down at the fire. How on earth could he be so blind? Did he really not know why she was being defensive? Not realise the effect he was having on her? Or was he merely pretending not to notice for her sake? And, if he was, then it would be better to allow the fiction. Pretending to consider his question, she pursed her lips thoughtfully. 'I don't know that I'm defensive exactly, I think it's more that I'm a private sort of person. I don't go around telling all and sundry about myself. . .'

'Unlike me, do you mean?' he asked with a wry smile.

'No.' Turning her face towards him, she tried to echo his smile. 'No, I think perhaps in your case there were extenuating circumstances.' Recalling his withdrawal in the pub, his accusations, she decided that perhaps it might be wise to change the subject. Nodding towards his bandaged hand, which he was cradling against his chest, she asked, 'How is it?'

'Sore,' he said succinctly. 'You don't realise how much you need two hands until one is inoperative. You can't get lids off jars! Can't shave properly——'

'Drive,' she put in naughtily.

'Mmm.' His eyes unexpectedly holding hers, he put out his hand and twisted a curl of her hair round his finger. 'It's gone into ringlets.'

'Yes,' she whispered as her breath lodged somewhere in her throat. Hastily moving her head away, she babbled, 'It always does when it gets wet.' Without a brush to ruthlessly suppress it, it stuck out like a bush, and, forgetting her attire for a moment, she put both hands up to flatten it then had to make a hasty grab for the sheet. Catching the edge of his grin, she looked hurriedly away.

'Do you have any idea how provocative you look?' he teased mildly.

'About as provocative as you, no doubt,' she returned flatly. Please don't do this to me, she wanted to beg. I'm trying so damned hard to stifle my awareness of you, of the fact that beneath the sheet you're naked. That I'm naked. With a hastily suppressed groan, she stared frantically down—at long, tanned legs lying side by side with her own. He had nice legs. Had a nice body, come to that. Narrow hips, hard flat stomach—oh, God, Neile, stop it!

Becoming aware that he was observing her appraisal,

she blushed scarlet, and was inordinately thankful when Mrs Goff bustled in to sever the awkward moment.

Turning towards her, Mackenzie smiled and sniffed appreciatively as he took the laden tray from her. 'That looks nice, thank you.'

'Only soup and bread, I'm afraid, but it will warm you both. Now you get tucked into that and I'll see about drying those clothes of yours.' With a smile for them both, she went back to the kitchen.

Dry them quickly, Neile prayed.

'Shift nearer,' Mackenzie said. 'I can then balance the tray between us so that we can both reach.'

'I can reach fine,' she exclaimed hastily.

'Neile,' he said warningly, 'shift nearer.'

Neile shifted, then started as her thigh came into contact with his, and, praying he wouldn't comment, made a great fuss out of breaking a slice of bread into small pieces.

'Don't like being touched, Neile?' he commented softly and she gave an exasperated sigh.

'I might have known you'd make a production out of it! All I did was start!'

'I know. I just wondered why. In the car, if I accidentally touched you, you flinched away——'

'Well, that's a normal reaction, isn't it? You are a stranger, after all——'

'And strangers are in the habit of touching you, are they?'

'No! Yes! Oh, for goodness' sake eat your soup!' And yet, even though he did as she asked, it didn't take away the tension, the fraughtness.

Picking up his spoon he began to eat, then sighed deeply. 'I'm sorry, Neile, I didn't mean to make you uncomfortable, or take my frustration out on you, it's just that I feel so damned helpless! I hate taking him back to her! She's so damned unpredictable!'

A little startled by the sudden change of topic, but

inordinately grateful all the same, she asked worriedly, 'She won't harm him, will she?'

'Not physically, no, of course she won't. But mentally? I wish I knew.'

'Doesn't he tell you? I mean, if he's unhappy with her?'

'No. He doesn't say very much at all.' With another long sigh, he asked unexpectedly, 'Have you ever been in love, Neile? Really in love, with a gut-wrenching emotion that saps the will? Leaves you helpless and without direction?'

Searching his face as he stared rather blindly at the fire, she shook her head before admitting quietly, 'No. Not like that. Considering the erratic temper Ellen says I have, it's perhaps surprising, but no, I've never met anyone who caused that reaction.' Yet was that really true? she wondered. It hadn't exactly been a conflagration with Gordon, but she had loved him, had thought he loved her until he had brutally shattered her illusions.

'It's like being set on fire, an all-consuming blaze that leaves no room for reason.'

'And burns itself out as quickly?'

'Not quickly, no. I could have wished it had,' he whispered reflectively as he transferred his gaze to his half-finished soup. 'I met Caroline when I was twenty-five, ten years ago—ten lifetimes ago. I had my life all planned out, so sure in my arrogance where I was going. It came as such a shock meeting her. I'd always been in control, never involved with the women I'd been out with, it was just. . .'

'Expediency?' she asked with a faint trace of bitterness that he didn't seem to notice. 'A relieving of sexual tension?'

'Perhaps,' he agreed moodily.

'And now you're getting divorced.'

'Mmm,' he agreed with a cynical twist to his mouth. 'We are currently going through the wonderful process of division of property and how much money she can screw out of me.'

'All because you once loved her and now no longer do?' she queried. 'A woman scorned and all that?'

'Maybe. Hard to see now how that bitter-tongued shrew was once loving. Hard to remember she was once faithful.'

His anger seemed directed more towards himself than his ex-wife—because he'd been duped? she wondered. Played for a fool? Or because the fire hadn't burned out and he still loved her? 'And Daniel? Is he being fought over too?'

'Oh, yes,' he said bitterly. 'If we can agree on a settlement, she will generously allow me to have Daniel. If not, she will keep him and make his life a misery. He's a pawn, Neile, a pawn in a game in which my hands are bloody tied! How can you use your own son as a chess-piece?' With an irritable twitch of his shoulders, he continued with his meal.

No wonder Daniel had been so unhappy, and she hadn't helped, she thought guiltily, reproving him the way she had. Yet how could she have known? Poor Daniel, poor Mackenzie. Staring at his strong face, she wondered why he had confided in her. Not for her sympathy, or understanding, she didn't think; perhaps just because he needed to talk, put it into words. 'Are you going to give in over Daniel?'

'What else can I do? You saw how he was—he's hardly an advert for a well-adjusted child, is he?'

'No,' she agreed lamely, and wished in a way that he hadn't confided in her—because it made them no longer strangers, and remaining strangers would be so very much safer. Especially during the coming night.

CHAPTER THREE

THOUGHTFULLY finishing her own soup, Neile put her spoon tidily in the dish and leaned back. She didn't want to get involved with this man. Didn't want to get involved with any man, she thought with a wry twist to her mouth. It was barely three months since Gordon's betrayal, far too soon to be thinking about getting involved again; then she gave a faint smile at her own conceit. It was very doubtful Mackenzie would want to get involved again either after his disastrous marriage. 'Finished?' she asked quietly as he too leaned back.

'Mmm. Thanks.'

'Then I'll take the tray out.' Standing, hitching her sheet firmly, she picked up the tray and went out to the kitchen. With a faint smile at Mrs Goff, she put it on the draining-board. 'Thank you, that was lovely.'

'You're welcome, dear. Now, if I put them on the tray, can you carry the coffee-pot and cups?' she asked as she turned the battered coffee-pot handle towards Neile. 'No milk, I'm afraid, till my daughter comes in the morning, but I've put sugar in the bowl. Now, the only spare blanket I have is this one,' she added as she indicated a woollen throwover on the back of the kitchen chair. 'I do hope you'll be warm enough, but if you keep the fire in it should be all right,' she said worriedly.

'The blanket will be fine—don't worry, please. We're just so grateful to you for letting us stay.'

'Oh, no need for thanks. I wouldn't leave a dog out on a night like this. Brenda should be here around seven and she'll be more than happy to drive your man to the garage. Now, I keep early hours here, so if you don't mind I'll go on up. Make sure you put the lamp out, won't you?'

'Yes, of course.'

'Right, I'm off to bed, then. Goodnight, lass.'

'Goodnight.'

Throwing the blanket over one shoulder, she picked up the tray and, taking a deep, calming breath, returned to the disturbing Mackenzie and the rather alarming prospect of having to sleep with him. You're wearing a sheet, Neile, she told herself firmly. He's wearing a sheet. You've have a blanket; not the least need to get in a lather just because you have to share the sofa with him. She didn't even really know why she found him so disturbing. He'd made it quite clear that he wasn't interested—only her experience of men in the past didn't exactly give her the comfort she sought. Since the age of fourteen she seemed to have been fighting off unwelcome attentions with more and more desperation. But not Mackenzie, she told herself firmly.

With an irritable shrug of her shoulders, she decided to take things as they came. Not much else she could do. Kicking the door open, she edged through then smiled her thanks as Mackenzie got swiftly to his feet and relieved her of the tray. And, if her smile was a little wan, Mackenzie was kind enough not to comment on it.

'Thanks. Mrs Goff has gone to bed and she said to make sure we put the lamp out before we—er—sleep.'

'OK. Did you find out where the facilities are?' he asked as he resumed his seat.

'Oh, damn. No, I forgot, although presumably in an old cottage this size they're outside.'

'Mmm, that's what I feared,' he agreed with a teasing smile. 'Oh, well, I'll have my coffee then investigate. Chivalry is not dead, you see.'

'I'm very glad to hear it, and if you meet any spiders I would be enormously grateful if you'd vanquish them. Dragons I can cope with. Spiders, most decidedly not!' she babbled. For some silly reason it seemed important not to have any long silences.

'Spiders?' he exclaimed with a horrified expression.

'Not me, lady, they terrify the life out of me. Spiders you will definitely have to deal with on your own!'

'You can't be terrified of spiders!' she retorted, her eyes full of disbelief. 'A great big lad like you?'

'What's size got to do with it?' Giving a theatrical shudder, he poured coffee for them both. 'Spiders frighten me to death! Especially those great black hairy ones—so, on second thoughts, I think you'd better investigate first. It's a well-known fact that women are far braver than men!'

'Well, that's true,' she confirmed, 'although so much for star signs,' she added with a rueful smile. 'Ariens are not supposed to be cowards.'

'Well, this one is, and not in the least ashamed to admit it. Drink your coffee—you'll no doubt need the fortification!'

Shaking her head at him, she sipped the hot brew, but wasn't in the least surprised when he began to push his feet into his boots and with a funny grimace got to his feet.

When he'd gone she stared at the small sofa and tried to tell herself that it would be all right. Mackenzie had already said she had nothing to fear, and she did believe him, only. . . Oh, for goodness' sake, Neile, you're twenty-seven, not a child! Impatient with herself, she got to her feet and spread the blanket across the couch. There. Not that they were likely to get much sleep. Mackenzie was broad and well over six feet and the sofa couldn't measure more than five, and although she wasn't exactly enormous she wasn't skinny or short either.

Needing something to do to take her mind off things, she put the cups on the tray and carried it out to the dark kitchen before hurrying back to the fire. Putting on another couple of logs to keep it in, she turned as Mackenzie hurried in, shaking himself like a dog.

'It's still pouring, I'm afraid, but I found this old mac in the kitchen which will at least keep the worst off you.

Here.' Holding it out, he draped it round her shoulders. 'I didn't hear any sinister rustlings so one can only hope that the spiders have gone to bed.'

'How far is it?' she asked tentatively as she wondered whether her need was that urgent. The thought of fumbling through a dark garden into an equally dark hut with possible resident wildlife didn't appeal at all, and she wished now that she hadn't drunk the coffee.

'Not far; you can see it quite easily. It's painted white, directly in line with the back door. There's even a path of sorts, although hellishly muddy.' When she still hesitated, he quipped, 'Want me to hold your hand?'

'I'm sorely tempted to take you up on that offer; however. . .' Perching on the sofa arm, she attempted to push her feet into her wet boots, then cursed as the lining caught on her bare feet.

'Here, use mine,' he offered. Treading them awkwardly off, he pushed them towards her.

Feeling a fool, she pushed her feet into them and shuffled out.

As he'd said, it was easy enough to find, but what he hadn't told her was that the facilities only consisted of a bucket. Refinements such as a seat were obviously considered unnecessary. Scurrying back to the cottage as fast as she could in the over-large boots, she quickly washed her hands in the kitchen, and, leaving the mac across the back of a chair, hurried through to the warmth of the lounge. Shivering, standing in front of the fire, her hands held out to the blaze, she stiffened as Mackenzie moved up behind her and proceeded to rub her cold arms with one warm palm.

The warmth of him at her back made her want to lean against him; the feel of his hand on her bare arm altered her breathing, and she prayed he wouldn't notice.

'You didn't mention the primitiveness of the arrangements,' she scolded huskily.

'I didn't dare,' he chuckled, and, seemingly quite

unaware that his touch was making her shiver more than the cold, he added gently, 'Feeling warmer now?'

'Yes, thanks.' Clearing a throat that felt somehow restricted, she moved away from him and gave a hesitant smile over her shoulder.

'You have realised, haven't you, that the sleeping arrangements are going to be somewhat. . .?'

'Intimate, yes,' she agreed quietly, 'but I don't think either of us would wish the other to try and sleep on that hard floor. We have a long trip ahead of us tomorrow.'

'Yes, we do.' Turning her gently round, he stared searchingly into her blue eyes. 'You have no need for concern, Neile. I shan't touch you.'

'No, I know. I'm just being silly—sorry.'

'Apology accepted. And just to prove how chivalrous I really am, I'll even give you a choice. Do you wish to sleep on the outside or inside?' he asked lightly.

'Oh, outside, I think.' That way if it became too unbearable she could escape more easily.

'Right, then. I'd best sleep this way in order to keep my bad hand uppermost.' Indicating what he meant, he pulled his sheet more firmly around him and settled himself as best he could on the short sofa, his legs hanging over the end.

Eyeing him nervously as he held up one edge of the blanket for her to slide in, her insides a churning mass of nerves, she turned out the lamp, then, adjusting her own sheet, she lay gingerly down in the narrow space remaining. As he shifted to accommodate her, he whispered naughtily in her ear, 'We'll have to play spoons.'

'No, Mackenzie,' she retorted firmly, 'we don't have to play anything. Just sleep.'

'Yes, ma'am. And Neile?'

Twisting her neck so that she could see his face, she asked warily, 'Yes?'

'I should have mentioned it before, but I told Mrs Goff that our names were Mr and Mrs Markham.'

'Markham? But why?'

'Because we are not a million miles from Caroline, and if she finds out that I've spent the night here with you, no matter how innocently, it will give her just one more lever to use against me.'

'It's not very likely she'll find out, is it?'

'Not very, no, but more unlikely things have happened. This is a small community and I don't imagine anything very much ever happens here, so when a couple of strangers, Southerners at that,' he explained ruefully, 'arrive out of the storm, I reckon Mrs Goff might talk it to death. Certainly she'll have to tell her daughter and they will speculate about it to their cronies, word will spread. . . I know it sounds inconceivable, but I know the gossip that goes on in these isolated places. It travels, grows, becomes eventually almost unrecognisable from the original tale.'

His voice was abrasive, slightly bitter, and Neile wondered what tales in the past had perhaps been spread about him. 'So, if it does happen as you say, all she'll know is that a young married couple named Markham spent the night?' she said.

'Yes. Do you mind?'

'No, no, I don't mind, it makes no difference to me, although it might have been better to use a name other than mine.'

'Yes,' he agreed with a rueful smile, 'but thinking on my feet when I'm wet, uncomfortable, tired and crabby was a feat beyond me. The only name I could think of on the spur of the moment was yours. OK?'

'Yes, OK,' she agreed quietly.

'And as I'd already noticed you wear a ring on that finger. . .' With a tired smile, he queried softly, 'Why do you wear it? To deter would-be suitors?'

'Not so much suitors, more as protection against unwelcome advances.'

'And do you get many? Yes,' he answered himself, 'I suppose you do. Looking like Snow White must be a distinct disadvantage.'

'It is. Walt Disney has a lot to answer for,' she quipped huskily. In the almost dark room his face looked softer, kinder, and she felt an odd churning inside her as unexpected as it was unwelcome. Turning over, presenting him once more with her back, she said firmly, 'Goodnight, Mackenzie.' Regrets for the road she had chosen were foolish. One day maybe she would meet someone who would value her for herself, for the person inside. Someone who could ignore the packaging. But not Mackenzie. He had enough troubles in his life and wasn't likely to welcome another commitment, or not for a very long time to come. Even if he liked her, which she wasn't sure he did, he wasn't free.

'Night,' he answered with a soft sigh.

Unbearably conscious of his warmth at her back, of the hard thighs tucked beneath her own, she lay rigid and stared at the fire. All the arguments in the world, all the comforting phrases she repeated to herself, didn't make one iota of difference to her feelings. One part of her wanted to turn into his embrace, snuggle against that strong body, and another part insisted that, if he so much as sighed differently, she'd kill him. Yet he wasn't immune, she knew he wasn't, his breathing was far too regular to be natural. It was the touching that was doing it; if she could somehow make space between them. . . On this tiny couch? Be sensible, Neile!

Conflicting emotions warring uncomfortably in her mind, she continued to lie rigid.

'Relax,' he instructed sternly, and the breath of his words stirred the hair at her nape, making her shiver.

'I can't. . . I'm not used. . . I don't find this easy, Mackenzie,' she admitted with an awful mixture of embarrassment and awareness.

'You think I do?' he asked, still in that same soft, almost deliberately neutral voice. A few seconds later, he gave a deep sigh before adding gruffly, 'I'm not made of stone.'

'No.' With a heavy sigh of her own, she tried to

unclench her muscles. Tried deep breathing; tried to relax each separate part of her; prayed for sleep.

She thought afterwards that it must have been the most uncomfortable night she had ever spent. Neither of them could get comfortable on the narrow couch, and every time she began to drift Mackenzie would move or mutter incomprehensibly, and she was wide awake again. Staring resentfully into the dying fire, she shifted crossly as his knee edged her further and further towards the floor. Her fingers desperately clenched in the edge of the cushion to stop herself falling, she pressed back with her hips, trying to win some room until with an irritable grunt he pushed back, reclaiming the ground she had won.

Unable to stand it any longer, she swung her feet to the floor and huddled miserably on the edge, her arms hugging her knees in an effort to keep warm, and any softening she might have felt towards him earlier was now totally dispelled. God, men were so selfish, even when they were asleep!

'What in heaven's name are you doing?' he complained irritably, his voice rough and sleep-thickened.

'I'm not doing anything,' she snapped back, 'except freezing to death!' When a strong arm encircled her and dragged her backwards to lie flat once more, she yelped in alarm and struggled futilely to be free.

'Lie still, damn you! How the hell can I sleep with you shifting prissily every five minutes?'

'I was not shifting prissily!' she grated furiously. 'I was trying to keep from falling off—and get your damned hands off me!' When he didn't immediately comply, she lashed out and accidentally caught his bad hand. 'Sorry,' she muttered when he gave an indrawn hiss of pain, 'but it's your own fault. How the hell can I sleep when you keep dragging the cover off me?'

'Right, that's it!' he said flatly. 'Come on—up.' Levering himself upright, pulling and urging her to do the same, he shoved her up one end of the sofa by the expedient method of using his feet. 'Now you sit at that end, I'll sit at this! And to hell with you, Neile bloody Markham!' With each of them curled uncomfortably at opposite ends, he spread the blanket across them. 'Now sleep!'

Glaring at him, she dragged the cover more up her end and curled into a resentful ball. Ignoring his muttered swearing, she held on tight to her end of the blanket. Arrogant, bloody-minded. . . No wonder his wife had left him! Shoving his cold foot off her shin she determinedly shut her eyes. If he thought he could evict her again, he was in for another think; in the mood she was in, she'd defend her bit of sofa to the death! Muttering and cursing to herself, she wriggled into a more comfortable position and rested her head on the sofa arm. 'And I'm not prissy!' she insisted crossly. He was probably so used to women hurling themselves at him that a little natural reticence, a few standards, just thoroughly confused him. Her lovely face set in a scowl, she screwed her eyes tight shut, and gradually, as exhaustion overtook her, she slowly drifted into a troubled doze.

In sleep their bodies relaxed and found more comfortable positions. Neile unconsciously stretched her legs out over him, and Mackenzie curved his body to accommodate hers until his foot accidentally prodded her in the ribs. Semi-awake, she rubbed her hand along the bare calf that was extended over the soft arm beside her face and only gradually became aware of what she was doing. Snatching her hand back as though stung, she opened her eyes. Blinking in the grey half-light of dawn, she groaned as she became aware of the stiffness in her back. Moving carefully so as not to wake him, she stared along their entwined lengths. Her lower limbs were hugged to his chest, her cold feet almost touching his nose, and she gave a sour grin. He was in for a shock if he suddenly woke up. He still had most of the sofa, she saw resentfully, then winced as cramp struck in her thigh. Rubbing awkwardly at the painful spot, she surveyed her companion. His injured hand was lying on top of the cover, the fingers loosely curled. His mouth was parted and breath was whistling noisily in and out, and despite herself she smiled. His dark hair curled untidily across his brow, dark stubble blurred the outline of his jaw. One broad shoulder was uncovered and every so often he gave a twitch as though even in sleep he was aware of the draught on his naked skin. Her hand had returned to his calf, she saw with surprise, and without even realising she was going to she began to smooth her hand back and forth across the muscle. His legs were surprisingly hairless for a dark man, warm and tanned, and the feel of warm skin beneath her hand was enormously pleasurable. It had been a long time since she'd felt the close warmth of another human being, and she missed it. Missed the companionship—no, that wasn't entirely true, she missed the companionship that she had wanted, had dreamed of, and never received. What was it about beauty that made other people assume you didn't need the ordinary things of life? A caring relationship; someone to lean on and be leaned on in return. Someone who would take the trouble to see who was inside. . .

For long moments, she watched him, fantasised even, because he was so very attractive, so very confident about himself, and whatever indefinable something that made him the man he was made her yearn for something more. What would it be like to be held by him? Kissed by him? Cherished? And oddly she didn't even need to wonder; she knew what it would be like, knew how she would feel. Her eyes pricking with tears for a dream that would in all probability never reach reality, she gave a long, unhappy sigh. If the circumstances had been different. . .

Peering at her watch, she saw it was barely five and, as she moved, her back gave a twinge of pain. Knowing she wouldn't be able to go back to sleep in this cramped position, she wondered if she could move without waking him. Cautiously withdrawing her feet, she slowly levered herself upright. Clutching the back of the sofa, she eased herself over the top. Careful not to make any sudden moves, she walked round to the front of the sofa and lowered herself into the small space left by his body. Curving herself along the line of his, she stiffened when he moved to accommodate her as though he was used to a woman curving against him. Which of course he was, and she wondered how long it had been since he'd slept with his wife. Drawing the cover carefully over her, she sighed in relief as the stiffness eased from her back and within minutes was fast asleep.

A loud bang woke her and her eyes snapped open in shock. Staring blankly before her, it took her a moment or two to reorientate herself, and she gave a little sigh that was echoed from behind her. As full memory rushed back, she turned her head and stared into light grey eyes that looked as bewildered as her own.

Flopping back down, he groaned. 'Oh, God, I feel as though I've been beaten all over. Did we sleep?'

'Well, you did, certainly,' she said tartly.

'Oh, my, we are full of sweetness and light this morning,' he muttered irritably. 'What time is it?'

Dragging her arm out, she stared at her watch. 'Six-thirty.' Remembering her move in the night, she complained softly, 'I've only had a couple of hours' sleep!'

'Then get some more now! I'll get up—if I can get up,' he amended with another groan. 'I think my legs have got frostbite.'

'Well, if you're about to complain that I had all the cover, don't,' she warned, feeling decidedly irritable and out of sorts. Trying to move, she found she couldn't and that Mackenzie was lying on her sheet, effectively trapping her. There also seemed to be rather too much flesh meeting flesh for her liking and she wriggled impatiently, trying to get free.

'Now what are you doing?'

'You're lying on my sheet!'

'Oh, good grief!' Bracing his neck on one sofa arm and his heels on the other, he arched upwards so that she could pull her cover free.

'Thank you!' Dragging the concealing folds round her, she crawled off the edge and got to her feet and then staggered and sat back down.

'Ouch!'

'Sorry,' she muttered grudgingly. Turning her head, she saw he had his eyes closed again. 'Don't go back to sleep! Mrs Goff will be down soon.'

'So?'

'So Brenda will be here.'

'Oh, b. . .' With a grumpy sigh, he levered himself into a sitting position and regarded her balefully. 'Are you always this bad-tempered in the mornings?'

'No. I'm stiff and I'm cold and I'm tired.'

'And grumpy,' he added with an unexpected grin, 'and quite astonishingly fanciable. If you could just curb this deplorable habit you have of bossiness——'

'And if men weren't so ineffectual, we women wouldn't need to be bossy,' she riposted sweetly. 'I'm going to see if our clothes are dry and get dressed before Brenda comes.' With an audible sniff she marched into the kitchen and quickly dressed in the stiff dry clothes. Once dressed, she felt more herself, and she lingered for a moment to stare from the kitchen window. She could recall very clearly the feeling of his warm flesh against her own, and she gave a little shudder. Then, remembering his words, she gave a small smile. Did she want to be fanciable? Yes, damn it, she did. She wanted. . . Snatching a deep breath, she picked up his clothes and returned to the lounge. He'd curled himself back on the sofa, the blanket pulled over his head, and just for a moment, just one little moment, she allowed herself a fond smile. He really was rather special, and perhaps, just perhaps. . . No, don't be dumb, Neile.'

'Mackenzie! Don't go back to sleep!'

'Oh, God,' he complained, his voice muffled, 'I pity any man you marry. He won't have a moment's peace.' With reluctant fingers, he dragged the blanket back down, then gave a grunt of laughter. 'You look like a very determined hedgehog! Feel better with your clothes on?' he teased gently.

Staring down at him, she gave a rueful smile. 'Yes. I'm not a very liberated lady, I guess.'

'No, not that that's anything to be ashamed of.'

'I know. Here, I brought your clothes in. Can you manage?'

With a distinctly wicked smile, he shook his head, his eyes full of laughter. 'Coward!' he called after her as she retreated to the kitchen.

With the door safely closed between them, she gave a rich chuckle. Wretched man. Hearing footsteps behind her, she smiled as Mrs Goff descended the little staircase that led down from her bedroom. 'Good morning.'

'Good morning, dear, how did you sleep?'

'Fine,' she lied, then laughed when Mrs Goff gave her an old-fashioned look.

'Well, let's get the kettle on, then at least you can both have a cup of tea when Brenda arrives. She shouldn't be long.'

Mackenzie had only just joined them in the kitchen when Mrs Goff's daughter arrived, and, once the situation had been explained to her, she was more than happy to oblige. Their tea drunk, Neile elected to go to the garage with Mackenzie, and thanking Mrs Goff warmly for her kindness, they went out into the chilly morning with Brenda.

The drive to the garage didn't take long and, while Mackenzie borrowed a can and filled it with petrol, Neile bought two large bunches of flowers from the service shop for Brenda and her mother. She also quickly used the garage facilities to wash and tidy herself before joining Mackenzie for the ride back to where they'd left the car.

'Cheat,' he taunted softly once they were on their way again, this time on the right road.

'Why?' she asked, puzzled.

'Because you look as fresh as when we started out yesterday and I feel like a tramp.'

Smiling, she denied, 'I don't feel fresh—but then neither do you look like a tramp. Just attractively rumpled. However, if you can direct us to somewhere that serves breakfast, I think we'll both feel a great deal better.'

An hour later they were back on the motorway and, as Neile had said, both felt better for having eaten. Mackenzie had also managed to buy a pack of disposable razors, and was now washed and shaved, and although they were both tired they were glad to be on their way home.

'May I ask you something?' she asked quietly as they drove steadily south, and when he nodded, continued, 'Why did you need to come by car?'

With a long sigh, he explained, 'Because Daniel gets train-sick. And boat-sick,' he added with a faint smile. 'And probably air-sick. The only way he can usually travel comfortably is by car. Don't ask me why; you'd think travel-sick was travel-sick was travel-sick. . .'

'Poor Daniel,' she commiserated softly. 'I hope it all works out for you.'

'Yeah. I'll let you know—if you'd like me to. . .'

'Yes, I would, thank you. He was a nice little boy.'

'Despite pulling your hair?' he teased.

'Did he tell you?' she asked, surprised.

'Yes. And about the deer and the painting. He said you were pretty. And so you are,' he added softly, 'and perhaps in different circumstances. . .'

'Only the circumstances aren't different. . .'

'No,' he agreed heavily. 'But in six months, a year, who knows?'

Glancing at him, seeing the faint smile in his light grey eyes, she smiled back. 'Yes,' she echoed, 'who knows?'

The rest of the journey was completed mostly in silence. Not a heavy or uncomfortable silence, just a tired quietness, and when she pulled up in his driveway and killed the engine both were reluctant to end it.

'Well, Neile Markham,' he finally exclaimed, 'end of the road.' Turning to face her, he trailed a gentle finger down her cheek. 'Time to say goodbye.'

'Yes,' she whispered, her beautiful dark blue eyes fixed on his face. 'Say hello to Daniel for me when you see him.'

'I will.'

'Will you be able to manage all right, with your hand and everything?'

'Mmm, I expect so. I can always get cabs till it's healed.'

'Will you stay here until then?'

'No, probably not. I only rented it for Daniel's sake, so that we could be together. For a bit of peace. I like this part of the world and it's far removed from Caroline. . .' Breaking off, he reached into the glove compartment and removed his cheque book. Opening it awkwardly on his knee, he quickly filled in one of the cheques. Then he tore it out and handed it to her.

'Not going to look at it?' he teased her, obviously amused when she merely folded it in half and tucked it into her pocket.

Shaking her head, she gave a sheepish smile. 'It always looks so rude to check an amount, sort of greedy or something.'

'Silly girl. You won't make a success of business that way.'

'No.' Then, with a funny little shrug, she said, 'Well, I suppose I'd better go in.'

'Yes.' Leaning forwards, he pressed a soft kiss on her parted mouth, and no doubt that was all he intended, a quick thank-you kiss. It came as much a surprise to her as she knew it did to him when her mouth softened and seemed to cling. With a little groan, he gathered her closer and kissed her properly, lingeringly. When he finally drew back, she stared at him, her eyes startled.

'Not intended, Neile,' he said softly, his eyes serious.

'I know,' she whispered.

'But nice, hmm?' he asked. As though unable to help himself, he trailed one finger across her lower lip, his eyes on his task.

'Yes,' she agreed huskily.

'Yes,' he echoed on a long sigh. A hint of laughter in his eyes, he teased, 'An Arien trait, is it?'

'Quite possibly,' she agreed softly.

'Mmm, what did you say you were? A Libran?'

'Yes.'

'Compatible, are they? Aries and Libra?'

'Yes, fire and air.'

'And you're the fire?' he asked with a gentle smile.

'No, you are.'

'Oh, dear, horrid thought—fire can't exist without air, can it? But air can exist very nicely on its own.'

'Exist, yes,' she agreed quietly, 'but it can get very lonely.'

'So can fires, Neile, so can fires. People only ever want to put them out.' Still watching her carefully, his voice very soft, he continued, 'I'm tempted to say something trite about saving your kisses for when I'm free, but that wouldn't be fair, would it? You're a nice lady, Neile.' Then, suddenly, without any warning, his face hardened. Flicking a finger dismissively against her chin, he added abruptly, 'Goodbye—take care.'

'Yes.' Bewildered by the sudden change in him, her eyes pricking, she unlatched her door and scrambled quickly out. 'Bye,' she whispered before hurrying across the drive towards Ellen's cottage. Taking a deep breath, she stood on the doorstep for a moment to collect herself, then pushed quickly inside. Why had he changed so abruptly? Because it was hopeless? And yet, only a few hours before he had dismissed her, he'd spoken as though they might get together when his problems were all resolved. Six months, he'd said. Or a year. That wasn't so long, was it? She barely knew him, and yet she felt as though she had known him forever, and she'd have been lying if she said she didn't want to see him again, because she did. Very much. And yet not three months ago, when Gordon had walked out on her, she'd promised herself she was off men for good. And now she wanted a man she wasn't sure wanted her.

CHAPTER FOUR

NEILE spent the night with her mother, then drove back to London early the next morning. Struggling breathlessly up the three narrow flights of stairs to her office, she pushed open the door and smiled warmly at the brown-haired young woman already seated at her desk. No matter how early Neile was, Thelma was always there before her.

'Hi,' Thelma greeted with a faint smile. 'Have a good weekend?'

'So-so. Different, at any rate.' Hanging her coat on the rack, she rummaged in her bag and produced the cheque Mackenzie had given her. 'I also earned some money.'

'Neile!' Thelma exclaimed in laughing shock. 'You never charged your mother for painting her kitchen!'

'No, silly. I did a bit of unexpected temping—not that sort of temping!' she retorted disgustedly as Thelma collapsed in helpless laughter. 'Chauffeuring.'

'Chauffeuring? In that old buggy of yours?'

'There is nothing wrong with that old buggy, as you call it,' she reproved loftily, 'but no, as it happens—in his. Mother's new neighbour asked me to drive him up to Yorkshire.' Quickly explaining, or as much as she considered relevant for Thelma to know, she continued on her way to her desk. She didn't want to discuss her feelings with her friend; they were somehow too personal and private. 'Anything in the post?' she asked quickly.

'Not up yet,' Thelma said carelessly, then, tilting her head in a listening attitude, she smiled. 'Although if I don't miss my guess, that sounds remarkably like elephant boy coming now.'

'Careful!' Neile warned as Dennis, the office boy from

downstairs, erupted into the office nearly shattering the glass panel in their door. 'Otherwise your next week's wages will go on replacement glass!'

'Sorry, Neile,' he said perfunctorily, his young face split with a wide grin.

'Neile,' she corrected wryly, as she always corrected and which obviously went in one ear and out the other. 'It's pronounced Neeley.'

'Neile,' he corrected with a cheeky smile. 'I brought your post. Nothing interesting-looking.'

'Thank you, Dennis,' she said drily as she relieved him of the letters before he could actually open them, which she wouldn't have put past him. 'Goodbye,' she added firmly when he looked inclined to linger.

With a broad wink, he crashed back out again, slamming the door behind him, and both women winced.

'If that child works here much longer, there won't be any building left!' Neile muttered as she swiftly slit open the post.

'Bills outnumber requests again?' Thelma queried as she correctly interpreted Neile's sour expression.

"Fraid so.' Tossing the opened letters on to her desk, she propped her elbows on her typewriter and regarded her friend over her steepled fingers. 'Do you regret it?' she asked quietly, her face serious.

'Coming in with you? No. We'll make money, Neile— eventually.'

'Yes, but how long is eventually?' she asked despondently. Staring at her friend, her gaze distant, she suddenly asked, 'Thelma? Would you say I was bossy?'

'Bossy?' she queried slowly. 'No, not really. Forceful, perhaps—positive. Why?'

'Oh, no reason, I just wondered; but that's sort of bossy, isn't it? Being forceful? Do I boss you about?'

'If you hadn't,' Thelma pointed out wryly, 'I'd still be at home worrying about the gas bill.'

'You're still worrying about the gas bill——'

'Yes, but not at home! Don't get cold feet now,

Neile—it *will* work. It has to! Besides, my children would never forgive me if I threw the towel in now. They expect me to be rich and famous!' Her head on one side, she regarded her friend with sympathetic eyes. 'Why the sudden need for reassurance, Neile? Someone been getting at you?'

'No, not really. I just wondered. We don't always see ourselves as others see us, do we? It's funny, isn't it?' she murmured reflectively. 'Just because I look like stupid Snow White people either assume I'm dumb or promiscuous——'

'And because I'm plain,' Thelma put in, then repeated it firmly when Neile made a sound of protest, 'because I'm plain, people either pity me, assuming my mind is equally plain, or that I've latched on to you as a sort of compensation. Do you remember all the stick I took at school? Why do people find it so incomprehensible that someone astonishingly beautiful could want to be friends with a pudding?'

'And vice versa,' Neile added with a grin.

'Mmm. To be an extreme ain't easy. If you're ordinary, passably pretty, no one is astonished when you do anything—it's accepted. But if you're exceptional, in either direction, it suddenly becomes incomprehensible. So I know why you're sometimes aggressive: you feel you have to constantly prove yourself. That you're not a beautiful parasite but a hard-headed businesswoman.'

'Who is deeply in debt. Oh, well.' Pushing her troubles to the back of her mind, Neile got on with her work, and for the next week concentrated on getting their name known, even if her attention did wander more often than it should into thoughts of Mackenzie. Odd how she could remember every exchange they'd had. His expressions, the way he looked. . . She'd also gone over and over his parting words to her, trying to understand his abruptness at the end. Fire and ice, Ellen had said about Ariens, and, recalling his warmth one minute, his withdrawal the next, perhaps that explained it. And what had he really meant about people always wanting to put out fires? Had he meant his wife? Had she not wanted him fiery? Passionate?

With a long sigh and a rueful grimace for her preoccupation with a man she might never meet again, she made a determined effort to be conscientious. Advertising, that was the thing. If you could afford it. Staring at their headed notepaper, at the confident slogan, 'People, an Agency for People who need People', all she had to do, she thought wryly, was let the people know. Perhaps they could employ a bell-ringer. A Proclamation by Royal Decree! With a faint smile for her foolishness, she bent her attention to answering the few enquiries that they did have.

Talk of defeat wasn't mentioned again as both tried to fire the other with unbridled optimism, and by the start of the following week there was something else to talk about. A sharp rap on the door made them both look up; it was a sufficiently unusual occurrence as to cause them to glance at each other in surprised speculation. Clearing her throat, Neile called hesitantly, 'Come in.'

The vision of loveliness that entered caused them even more astonishment and had the unfortunate effect of making their shabby little office look positively condemnable. Sitting up straighter in an effort to at least give an impression of efficiency, Neile smiled politely. 'Can I help you?'

'Miss Markham?'

'Yes,' Neile admitted cautiously.

As the woman advanced further into the room, a smile on her exquisite face, Neile saw that she wasn't alone. A short, rather nondescript man accompanied her. Limp brown hair fell over his bony forehead when he gave a perfunctory nod.

'I wanted to thank you,' the vision declared, 'for looking after Daniel so kindly.'

'Daniel?' Neile queried blankly.

'My son. I'm Caroline Grant.' Then she added with curious emphasis, 'Mackenzie's wife.'

'Oh.' Totally nonplussed, she added lamely, 'Hello. Won't you sit down? Can I get you a cup of tea or something?' Her mind racing, she wondered why on earth Mackenzie's wife would come to see her. Thanking her for looking after her son seemed a rather lame excuse.

Refusing refreshment, Caroline perched daintily on the chair in front of Neile's desk. Raising dark brown eyes, which were in such contrast to her blonde curly hair, she smiled. 'You look surprised.'

'Well, yes, I am rather——'

'No matter what Mackenzie might have said, or led you to believe, I still love him. He's not the easiest man to know, but I do love him, Miss Markham,' she said earnestly, and she sounded so sincere that Neile frowned in puzzlement.

'I'm sorry, but am I being stupid?' Neile asked blankly, and, hardly liking to say that that wasn't the impression her husband had given, continued, 'I mean, I don't understand why you're telling me. I barely know your husband. All I did was drive him up to Yorkshire. . .' And become very, very attracted to him. Aching for a might-have-been that was rapidly receding, she wondered if Caroline did still love him. Even more importantly, did Mackenzie still love his wife? She had sometimes gained the impression that he did, and that his bitterness stemmed from this woman's infidelity.

'And spent the night with him on the way back?' Caroline put in softly.

Her mouth practically hanging open, Neile floundered, 'It wasn't—didn't——'

'Didn't spend the night together in an isolated cottage?'

'Well, yes, but not—er—intimately or anything. We ran out of petrol. . .'

With a tinkling little laugh that grated rather severely on Neile's nerves, Caroline wagged an admonitory finger.

'You seriously expect me to believe, Miss Markham, that my husband didn't make a pass at you?'

Finally gathering her scattered wits, she insisted firmly, 'Yes, because he didn't. I told you, we ran out of petrol, sought assistance at an isolated cottage, and because there wasn't a garage near by were forced to stay the night. That is all that happened and I rather resent your implication that I'm some sort of—floozie!' she finished, unable to think of an appropriate word.

'I didn't accuse you of anything, Miss Markham. Certainly not of being a—um—floozie! I was merely rather incredulous that my super stud husband, who has a known proclivity for the opposite sex, didn't make a pass at such an attractive girl——'

'Woman,' Neile corrected absently, 'and, whether your husband has a proclivity or not, he certainly didn't make a pass at me. In fact as far as I can recall we spent most of the time we were together arguing!' When Caroline only continued to look disbelieving and showed no obvious intention of terminating the meeting, Neile matched her stare for stare, her mind racing. How the hell did the damned woman find out about the cottage? Gossip, as Mackenzie had speculated? Did Caroline also know the name they'd used? But why had she come? Because she really did want Mackenzie back? Or was she trying to find a weapon to use against him? And if she was? Oh, hell. Determined that she wasn't going to find it through her, Neile tilted her head in unconscious arrogance, and, with some muddled idea of protecting him, she reiterated coldly, 'Far from being the Don Juan you evidently seem to think him, Mrs Grant, his behaviour towards me was gentlemanly in the extreme—well, no, not gentlemanly,' she corrected honestly, 'more indifferent, and at times was both boorish and sarcastic! And as for making a pass at me, that's ludicrous! I found him a cold, passionless man—for which I was extremely thankful,' she tacked on just in case Caroline should get the idea that she'd resented it.

'Hardly a fit person to care for a four-year-old boy, in fact. I mean, cold and passionless doesn't sound the sort of character to bother with a child's needs, does it?'

'I didn't say he was cold and passionless with Daniel!' Neile exclaimed in horror. 'I said he behaved that way towards me—a different thing entirely! Just what is it that you're trying to prove? That Mackenzie is an unfit father? Or husband?'

'Neither, Miss Markham,' she said softly, and with every appearance of sincerity. 'I told you, I want him back.' Getting to her feet, she straightened her slim shoulders and stared rather defiantly at Neile. 'You think I like using these methods? I don't, but I love him—and I want him back.'

Glancing over her shoulder at her companion, she asked quietly, 'Get it all, Donald?'

'Yes.' With a nasty smile at Neile, he snapped shut the little book he had been so busily writing in, held open the door for Caroline, and they both went out.

Feeling sick and shaken, bewildered and hurt, Neile got slowly to her feet, her eyes still fixed on the door. With a funny little shudder, she walked unsteadily across to the window and looked out. Staring down into the street, hardly even registering what she saw, she castigated herself bitterly for being such a fool.

'What was that all about?' Thelma asked quietly.

Turning a troubled gaze on her friend, she shook her head. 'I'm not sure, but I think I've just been extremely stupid. What do you think she was up to?'

'Doesn't take much intelligence to guess,' Thelma said quietly. 'Although, to be fair, one look at you would send any self-respecting neglected wife to the nearest lawyer.'

'What?' Neile asked blankly. 'No,' she denied faintly, 'that wasn't it.' Or was it?

'Wasn't it? I suspect it was,' Thelma said gently. 'You shouldn't take words at face value, you know; shouldn't be so trusting. You never see any bad in anyone until you're hit over the head with proof of their evil intent. I don't know what happened between you and Mackenzie, neither do I want to,' she added hastily, 'but if that woman had really wanted him back it would have made more sense for her to have gone to talk to him, not you. On the other hand, if she has seen him, maybe she just wanted to find out what you were like, what sort of threat you were likely to be. Although why she mentioned him being unfair to their son, I haven't quite figured out,' she added with an air of perplexity.

Remembering Mackenzie's explanation, his bitterness, Neile murmured, 'It wasn't anything to do with me, I don't think. I think she was trying to find grounds for upping the settlement. It's not funny!' she reproved as Thelma spluttered with laughter. 'Mackenzie said she wanted to bleed him dry. All she has to do is threaten to give evidence of his infidelity—or supposed infidelity—and he won't have a snowball's chance in hell.'

'Perhaps it's happened before,' Thelma said sagely, 'but, whatever the reason, I don't think it works quite like that. . .'

'It doesn't matter whether it does or it doesn't,' she argued, 'that's what she's playing at—I think.' And, as for its having happened before, that wasn't something she wanted to dwell on at all! Refusing to even allow herself to admit to the possibility, she continued staunchly, 'She doesn't want Daniel herself, only to make Mackenzie pay more to keep him! He had to be careful of his reputation, he told me that,' she insisted. 'But why would she keep telling me that she loved him and wanted him back? That doesn't make sense.'

'Perhaps it's true. Perhaps he was the one who insisted on a divorce, and she's using every damned weapon she can find to force him back. . . Was he the sort of man one would want back?' Thelma asked softly. 'Yes, I can see by your face that he was. Oh, Neile, what have you gone and done now?'

'Nothing.' Oh, Thelma, she added silently as she

stared at her friend, I know it sounds daft, but I think I fell in love with him. Or fell in love with what you thought was him? a hateful inner voice whispered. Was that it? she wondered unhappily. Had she been so very wrong about him? Was he a womaniser as Caroline had said? No, she wouldn't, couldn't believe that, but she wasn't totally sure she didn't believe that Caroline still loved him. And maybe, maybe his feelings for his wife weren't as dead as he had led her to believe. 'I have to find him,' she suddenly stated, 'explain what's happened.' Staring helplessly round her as though the shabby office might hold a clue, she asked worriedly, 'But where?'

Walking agitatedly back and forth, her brow puckered in thought, she suddenly snapped her fingers. 'Mother! She might know!' Perching on the edge of Thelma's desk, she picked up the phone and swiftly punched out the number. Tapping her fingers impatiently on the edge of the desk as it rang and rang, she muttered, 'Come on, come on,' then slammed it down in temper when it became obvious no one was going to answer it. 'Damned woman's never there when you want her!' she grumbled irritably.

'Just drove him up to Yorkshire, did you?' Thelma asked softly, her eyes alight with amusement.

'Yes! And you can take that look off your face for a start, Thelma Davies! Nothing happened. It didn't!' she stated forcefully. 'We merely ran out of petrol and stayed at a cottage.' Giving Thelma a snort of disgust when she chuckled, she went back to her own desk and threw herself moodily into the chair. 'Now where do I try?'

'Telephone directory?' Thelma asked helpfully.

'I can try, I suppose,' she muttered without much hope. 'He wasn't staying in Sussex, not for long anyway. I suppose he might just still be there.'

Leaning backwards she picked up the directory from the shelf behind her, only to fling it back, when Thelma said apologetically, 'Wasn't he just renting it?'

'Yes. So? Oh, knickers. So it won't be in his name, will it? And I haven't the faintest idea where he lives normally.' Grabbing the London directory, she spent a fruitless couple of hours ringing every M. Grant listed, to absolutely no avail.

'Perhaps he'll contact you?' Thelma comforted.

'Yes, and perhaps he won't!'

'Well, I don't know why you're getting yourself in such a state! Mackenzie sounds more than capable of sorting out his own problems, apart from which you didn't give anything away that she didn't already know——'

'Guessed!' Neile retorted. 'She was guessing, and big mouth confirmed it!'

'You don't know that,' Thelma pointed out gently.

'Yes, I do! Why else would she come? Because she didn't know for sure, that's why! Oh, Thelma, don't you see? If I could find him, I could warn him and he might be able to do something about it.'

'What?' Thelma asked sceptically. 'Deny it? Personally I think you're making a mountain out of a molehill, but I'd dearly love to know just what did go on in Yorkshire. I've never seen you so distracted, and especially not over a man.'

'Nothing happened in Yorkshire!' she denied irritably.

'And nothing's going to happen now,' Thelma soothed. 'It will sort itself out, you'll see.'

Only it didn't—or perhaps it did, only not the way Neile could have wanted. Two days later they had another visitor: Mackenzie himself, and the sheer control of the man was far more frightening than if he'd erupted into the office in temper. He didn't, just quietly opened the door and stood there, his face hard, his eyes narrowed. He was wearing a grey three-piece suit, immaculate and businesslike, and he looked unfamiliar, a stranger, intimidating.

Swallowing her uncertainty, Neile got slowly to her

feet. 'Oh, Mackenzie,' she exclaimed through a throat gone dry, 'I've been looking everywhere for you.'

'No doubt,' he said icily. Removing his gaze from Neile, he stared at Thelma then held the door pointedly open. 'I'm sure you have shopping to do, Mrs Davies, or lunch or something, don't you?'

'Yes, of course,' Thelma agreed, her voice flustered. Lunging to her feet, she grabbed her coat from the peg and fled. Mackenzie closed the door very quietly behind her and leaned against it.

'How do you know her name?' Neile asked with total inconsequentiality.

'How isn't important. You once told me that being unwanted hadn't affected you, but it was a lie, wasn't it? Being unwanted made you grasping and greedy. I wonder how it will affect Daniel?'

'You've seen Caroline,' she said flatly.

'Yes.'

Sighing, she stared at him helplessly. 'What did she——?'

'Be quiet,' he said quietly, without expression. 'Will he become a cheat? Resentful of everyone and everything? Or will he grow inward? Become even more introverted? Did you consider any of that, I wonder?'

'Mackenzie——'

'I said be quiet. All you had to do was ask me for more money when I gave you the cheque—I would have paid it, you know. Reluctantly, disgustedly, but I would have paid what you asked. But it was better this way, wasn't it? To tell my darling wife——'

'I didn't!' she exclaimed in exasperation. 'I know how it looks, but she took me by surprise, asking about you and everything. . .'

'Yes, Caroline likes to take people by surprise. Make an impact. Did you have a nice girlish gossip about me?'

'No!'

'Did she pay you? How much was I worth, Neile? One hundred, two?'

'She didn't pay me anything, dammit! She wheedled and insinuated——'

'And persuaded you to tell her what a terrible father I would make. Yes, I know. I've just come from a meeting with her and the lawyers.'

'It wasn't like that! Mackenzie, please, just let me explain——'

'I don't need you to explain.' Dipping his hand into his top pocket, he took out a small card and tossed it on to her desk. 'Caroline's lawyers—no doubt you will want to ring them if you think of any other juicy titbits to tell them; only remember that any further information has to be filed within the next few days. I trusted you,' he added, his eyes bleak and empty. 'And it hurts, Neile, that I could be so wrong about someone again.' Turning on his heel, he opened the door and left.

'No! Mackenzie!' she yelled. Scrambling hastily to her feet, she chased after him. 'Mackenzie!' Clattering down the stairs to the street, she was just in time to see him climb behind the wheel of his car. Dashing across the crowded pavement, she tried to wrench open his door. Without looking at her, he pressed the electronic lock and pulled away.

'Mackenzie! Oh—damn!' she exploded. Standing on the pavement, she watched the car pull out into the traffic. Wanting to throw something, she swung round and nearly fell over Thelma. 'Did you see that?' she stormed. 'My God, why are men so monumentally stupid? Why can't they just damned well listen?'

'Because they always think they know best,' Thelma said soothingly. 'Come on, inside, I'll make us some tea.'

'Tea? What the hell do I want tea for? He wouldn't even listen!' she complained unhappily as Thelma urged her back inside. 'Wouldn't let me explain.'

'They never do, dear. Well, when he's calmed down, had time to think about it——'

'No. He won't come back,' she said despondently, her temper subsiding. 'I told myself and told myself that I wouldn't get involved with any more men. And what do I do?'

'I thought you barely knew him,' Thelma commented, tongue in cheek.

'I don't.'

'No, dear, that's why you're so upset. . .'

'Oh, shut up,' she said without heat. 'I liked him, you know.'

'So I gathered,' Thelma said drily.

'I'm going to ring those damned lawyers,' she threatened, 'give them a piece of my mind. Damned misinterpretation, that's what it was! It's probably totally illegal——'

'Neile——'

'Well, it is. Coming in here, shouting at me—well, it serves him right! If he couldn't be bothered to even listen. . . To hell with him. That's it! Finish, *finito*, The End!' Turning a defiant gaze on Thelma, her eyes showing a faint glint of tears, she commanded, 'Well, don't just stand there, where's my damned tea?'

With a little splutter of laughter, Thelma went to put the kettle on.

Easy to say, Neile thought later that night as she lay in bed, hands linked behind her head, that it was finished, only she couldn't get it out of her mind. His face, his words, the implications. It was so unfair, so hurtful that he could misjudge her so. Why did men have to be so damned unreasonable? All her adult life she'd had hassle with men, even Gordon, who'd professed to love her, who'd skilfully worn down her distrust, her resistance, until she'd admitted how she felt about him, and then not a month later had told her he couldn't cope any more. *He* couldn't cope! Just because he couldn't handle other men's mocking remarks; their lewd jests, crude suggestions. My God, she'd been dealing with them all her life! Why did it have to matter what she damned well looked like? Well, sod the lot of them! Thumping over in the narrow bed, she buried her face in the pillow. She'd do what she'd promised herself she'd do: concentrate on the agency and to hell with everything else.

She might even have managed it if she hadn't noticed the small paragraph tucked at the bottom of the society page in her newspaper a few days later.

Mackenzie Grant, wealthy financier, was seen boarding a flight for New York this morning. Kicking the dust of a messy divorce from his heels? Or merely hiding away for the six-week period until his Decree Absolute? His young son Daniel, over whom there has been such controversy, was not with him.

Did that mean he hadn't got custody of Daniel? she wondered. Frowning over it, she only gave half her mind to work, and the more she tried to push it out of her mind, the more it persisted in intruding. She kept getting visions of Daniel's solemn little face; his tears; his hurt. It began to haunt her, the thought of him being forced to live with Caroline. Forced to live with a woman he hated, Mackenzie had said, and although that was probably exaggeration it must have had some basis in truth, and Daniel had certainly been reluctant to go back to her. She wasn't stupid enough to believe that her few words with Caroline had totally affected the outcome, but it had been partly her fault, and if she'd been more careful. . .

For the next few weeks, she threw all her energies into improving the agency, yet still she was unable to forget him, his words as fresh in her mind as the day he had said them. Surely a man she barely knew shouldn't have this sort of impact on her? He seemed to be in her mind constantly, and even the fact that the agency was now beginning to pick up failed to banish him. Neither was she able to get Daniel's sad little face out of her mind, and with Christmas coming, a time for children, what sort of festive time was he going to have?

'Oh, Neile, I do wish you'd stop brooding,' Thelma exclaimed. 'You've been sighing and sighing all morning.'

'Sorry, it's because it's Christmas——'

'No, it isn't, it's because the six weeks mentioned in the paper have been and gone and you're wondering if he's back in England, and divorced! I wish you'd forget the damned man!'

'Yes,' she agreed despondently as she walked aimlessly across to the window. She wished she could too. 'I keep thinking about Daniel,' she explained. 'Your talking about what you'd bought your children, what you were doing over the holiday, made me wonder what sort of Christmas he would have.'

'I expect he'll be all right,' she comforted awkwardly. 'Children are very resilient, you know, and she *is* his mother. Mackenzie probably exaggerated because he wanted him.'

'Yeah.' The fact that Thelma only confirmed what she had been thinking should have comforted her, yet it didn't. Perversely it only seemed to make her brood about it more.

'Well, I'm going out to get some lunch. Do you want anything brought in?'

'A cheese sandwich will do,' she said absently as she stared down into the busy street.

She was still standing there nearly an hour later, her mind empty—until she saw a long, gleaming Jaguar. It was almost as though her thoughts had conjured him up, she thought with a sad smile. . . Her expression suddenly arrested, and without even thinking about what she was doing, she almost leapt away from the window and raced out and down the stairs.

Frantically scanning the passing traffic, she focused on the Jag. It was Mackenzie! She knew it was!

'What on earth are you doing?' Thelma exclaimed in astonishment as she came up beside Neile. 'You'll catch your death of cold!'

'It's Mackenzie!'

'What?'

'Mackenzie!' she yelled at the startled Thelma. 'There!' she exclaimed, pointing.

'Neile——'

'It is!' she insisted. 'Quick, have you got your keys on you?'

'What?'

'Keys! Car keys!' she said urgently.

'You're not going to follow him?' she asked in disbelief.

'No—yes. I don't know. What do you think?'

'I think you'd be a damned fool.'

'Yes.' Her eyes on the car as it halted at traffic-lights, she made up her mind. Right or wrong, she needed to see him. 'Please?' she begged as she swung back to her friend. 'Please?'

With a heavy sigh, Thelma handed over the keys. 'You don't even have a coat. . .' but she was talking to herself; Neile was already in the car and swerving out into the traffic.

Manoeuvring dangerously past a taxi that was going too slow for her liking, Neile edged into the lane in front of the traffic-lights, and as they changed to green she crossed her fingers on the wheel and sent up a little prayer that she wouldn't lose him.

She hadn't the faintest idea where she was going. Didn't have time to look for route signs; all her concentration was on not losing sight of the Jag. The traffic was appalling and she dared not get too far behind him, but neither did she dare drive on his tail in case he spotted her, although she did begin to wonder if he had when he led her a merry dance up the motorway. Thelma's old Escort didn't have half the power of his automatic and if the motorway hadn't been busy she would have lost him for sure. It was also drizzling with rain, and what with depleted vision, being dazzled by other people's head-lights and the spray thrown up on the road, she began to wonder if she was entirely sane.

When she noticed a sign for Windsor Safari Park, she became convinced she wasn't. Supposing he was going back to Yorkshire? Well, if he didn't turn off soon, she'd have to go back. Remembering that other fateful journey, she glanced hastily at the petrol gauge then gave a little sigh of relief as she saw it showed half full. She'd have to leave enough to get back to the office, otherwise she *would* be in the soup. She had no money on her, no credit card—then had her attention violently brought back to the present as the Jag shot across the slow lane and on to the slip road.

'Oh, God.' Hastily signalling, she pulled across to the inside. Narrowly missing the rear of the car just passing, she shut her eyes and swerved after the Jaguar. There was an ominous squealing of brakes from behind her, but she didn't dare slow to look, only pray that she hadn't caused an accident. Her heart beating in overdrive, she forced her racing pulse under control and drove after Mackenzie. Much more of this and she'd be a nervous wreck.

After ten fraught minutes of driving along country lanes, he suddenly pulled up and Neile had to brake hastily to avoid sailing past him. Quickly reversing, she scrunched down in her seat as he got out of his car. Carefully locking it, he pushed open a wooden gate and disappeared from sight. She felt like an idiot, but she got out and crept after him. Peering round the wet hedge, she saw him let himself into a rather decrepit-looking house. As soon as the front door had closed behind him, she straightened up. Right. Right what? she wondered. Oh, Neile, you have got to be stark, raving mad. Yeah. But, seeing as she'd got this far. . .

Walking back to Thelma's car, she locked it, then retraced her steps. Recalling all past wrongs, whether real or imagined, to bolster her flagging courage, she pushed open the gate.

CHAPTER FIVE

MUD sucking hungrily at her heels, Neile carefully negotiated the slippery path, and without giving herself time to change her mind knocked loudly on the front door. When nothing happened, she knocked again, then nearly overbalanced as the door was wrenched open. Staring at Mackenzie, she felt shock lance through her. She shouldn't have been shocked—his image had lived in her mind for weeks—yet how could she have forgotten the impact that silver eyes and a mocking mouth made? It seemed forever since she'd seen him, and yet it seemed no time at all. She didn't recall, until much later, that he had looked equally shocked.

'Hello,' she said inanely.

With a growl of disbelief, he demanded, 'What the hell are you doing here?'

'I want to talk to you——'

'Well, I don't want to talk to you!'

Knowing that if she wasn't quick he would shut the door on her, she slipped hurriedly past him and into the lounge on her left. She was astonished to find that she was shaking. Quickly shoving her trembling hands into her skirt pockets, she went to stand in front of the weak fire he'd obviously only just put a match to. Hearing the front door crash to, she winced.

'How the hell did you find me?'

'I followed you,' she admitted quietly, and before he could do any more demanding she rushed hurriedly on. 'I saw you drive past the office. You're a lousy driver, you know—you nearly caused a pile-up on the motorway with that reckless swerve.'

'With my what?'

'Reckless swerve,' she repeated nervously. 'Shooting across the slow lane like that——'

'Shooting. . .' Staring at her, his confusion gave way to tight, hard anger. 'Get out of here!' Striding over to her, he gripped her arm and yanked her towards the door. 'Out! And don't ever,' he spat brutally, 'come back!'

'No! And take your hands off me! I need to talk to you and I'm not going anywhere until I've explained. You came barging into my office, accused me of all sorts of things, and then didn't even have the courtesy to listen to my explanation!'

'Courtesy?' he asked in disbelief. 'Courtesy?'

'Yes, courtesy! Well, let me tell you, Mackenzie——'

'No, Miss Markham! Let me tell you——'

'No! I came to explain and explain I will!'

Releasing her so suddenly that she staggered off balance, he leaned against the door-jamb, folded his arms, and said softly, 'OK. Explain.'

Off balance both mentally and physically by his abrupt about-face, and by the anger and contempt that was radiating from him in waves, she tried to gather her scattered wits, then stamped her foot in frustration when he smiled nastily.

'Time's up, Miss Markham—goodbye.'

'Time's up, Miss Markham,' she mimicked. It had taken a lot of courage to come and see him, a lot of nerve, and he was looking at her as though she were a no-account tramp. Stiffening her spine, she faced him squarely. 'You really are a bastard, you know.'

'Why? I gave you a chance to explain——'

'No, you didn't! You gave me barely two seconds to marshal my thoughts—and now you've made me damn well forget what I was going to say!'

'If you need to rehearse your speech or make up a convincing argument, I don't want to hear it.'

'Yes, you do! My God, I've spent the last few weeks anguishing over it, worrying about it—and now you're damned well going to listen! Perhaps, too,' she continued more quietly, 'I needed to see you again to make me realise that you weren't—aren't—oh, I don't think I even care any more!' she exclaimed wretchedly. 'It's Daniel I feel sorry for!'

'Oh, is it? Is that why you made sure he'd go back to his mother?'

'I didn't! She came waltzing into——'

'I don't want to hear,' he denied coldly. Walking away from her, he went to stand before the fire. Legs apart, hands behind his back, he looked like some damned Olympian, and his eyes flickered distastefully over her before settling on her face.

Staring at him, hating him, she wanted to weep. For weeks she had imagined some day meeting him again—and none of the scenarios she had conjured up had been anything like this, but she couldn't go without finding out about Daniel. 'How is he?' she asked quietly.

'How do you expect him to be?' he returned, and his voice sounded almost conversational.

'I don't know, do I? That's partly why I came, to find out.'

'And you expect that I will tell you?'

'Hope,' she corrected with more patience than she would have thought herself capable of. 'It's been worrying me, haunting me really——'

'And that's the only reason you came?' he interrupted smoothly, his voice and emotions now totally under control. 'To enquire about Daniel?'

'No. I came to explain what really happened.'

'You did not wish to enquire into my own health? How I coped?'

'How you coped?' she echoed in confusion. 'Have you been ill?'

'Ill? No, not ill. But didn't your—er—haunting, cover my own circumstances? What your meddling did to me?'

'Did to you?'

'Yes, Miss Markham, to me. Did it not occur to that

fertile little mind of yours that I might also be the loser in the game you played?'

'It wasn't a game!' she exclaimed. 'If you'd only let me explain. . .'

Holding up his hand to halt the flow of words, he said coldly, 'Let me tell you something about financiers, Miss Markham. Financiers must be seen to be pure, as in driven snow, as in virginal. You are following me? Pure, Miss Markham, reputation unsullied—ah, I see comprehension dawning. Yes, Miss Markham,' he continued in that same hateful voice that was without inflexion, soft and not in the least menacing, unless one could see his face. Unfortunately Neile could see his face and suddenly felt sick. 'Just the slightest whiff of scandal,' he resumed, 'has the City running for cover to shun the unhappy recipient as though he had plague. And without clients, shall we say, financiers can no longer finance. Can they, Miss Markham?'

Shaking her head mutely, she licked dry lips and wished herself anywhere but there.

'And there was a whiff of scandal, wasn't there? About a certain little episode in Yorkshire? About how the minute I had returned Daniel to my wife I was off to spend the night with you? So you see, Miss Markham, why I asked if you had spared a thought for me.'

'Yes, I'm sorry,' she whispered numbly.

'Miss Markham is sorry,' he concurred sarcastically. 'Well, that of course makes me feel so very much better.'

'I *am* sorry!' she insisted. 'Desperately sorry, and if there were any way I could undo it, believe me I would. But there isn't!'

'Isn't there?' he asked silkily.

'No! And it wasn't altogether my fault! All right, all right,' she added hastily when he began to repudiate it, 'it was partly my fault, that was why I felt so guilty, why I needed to see you to explain, see if Daniel was all right.'

'Because it's been haunting you—yes, you said. Well,

no doubt you can be haunted some more by the desperate straits you've brought me to.'

'No! I don't believe you've been brought to anything by my. . .'

'Callousness?' he asked helpfully. 'Disloyalty? Meddling?'

'I wasn't callous! And how the hell was I to know that Caroline was such a bitch?' she demanded.

'Ah, justification——'

'No, it isn't!' she burst out hysterically. 'There is no justification, I know that, I was stupid and thoughtless, and I believed Caroline—until it was too late! And I didn't come here to justify myself, only to explain.'

'Which you have now done——'

'No, I haven't! Mackenzie! You can't just dismiss it without at least hearing my side!'

'Yes, I can, Miss Markham. I don't believe we have anything further to say to each other. Goodbye,' Turning away, he leaned his arms along the mantelpiece, presenting her with his broad back. The light from the fire threw his shadow behind him, engulfing her.

Feeling helpless and outmanoeuvred, she made one last attempt to get through to him. 'Won't you at least tell me about Daniel before I go?'

'No.'

Her shoulders slumping in defeat, she turned away. 'I am sorry, Mackenzie, my words to Caroline were only ever said with the best of intentions. . .'

'And we all know where they lead, don't we?' Drawing a deep breath as though he too had been holding himself in check, he turned his head. 'Not gone yet?' he asked nastily.

Throwing him a glance of dislike, she turned and went out. Fumbling with the heavy front door, she almost had it torn out of her hands by the wind that seemed to have increased tenfold since she had been inside. It was also pouring with rain. She had no coat, nothing. She was going to get absolutely soaked. With a little burst of temper, she turned to slam the door and dragged it towards her with such force that she lost her footing on the wet step. With a cry of alarm, arms windmilling frantically, she fell backwards, one foot twisted painfully beneath her.

Muttering every swear-word she could think of, cursing and sobbing as excruciating pain shot through her leg, she sat with it cradled against her before slowly levering herself upright. Standing on one foot, she leaned weakly back against the door. Oh, God, please don't let it be broken, she prayed, because if it was she didn't think Mackenzie would help her. Despite the cold and rain lashing her, she felt clammy and slightly sick. Swallowing hard to combat the nausea, she gingerly lowered her foot only to snatch it hastily back as the same pain lanced through it.

Whimpering, close to tears, she stared at the gate. Such a short distance, really, she thought pathetically, only how the hell was she to get there? Maybe if she kept still for a moment the pain would go away. Maybe it was just a sprain. And if it wasn't? Well, if it wasn't, it wasn't, she thought impatiently, but she sure as hell couldn't stand here all night.

Her face set, she straightened and launched herself at the hedge. Maybe she could hop back to the car.

'What the hell are you playing at now?' Mackenzie demanded furiously from behind her.

'I'm not playing at anything!' she denied bitterly. 'I fell on your damned step!'

'So sue me, why don't you?' he grated acerbically. With a muttered curse, he strode across to her and caught her elbow in a vice-like grip.

'I can manage, damn you! Or were you intending to break my arm as well?' Trying to wrench herself free and keep her grip on the hedge at the same time, all she succeeded in doing was to fall against him as her good foot slithered off sideways on the muddy ground. Slumping defeatedly, she wanted to pummel him with her fists, rant and rail in frustration at being in such a stupid predicament. Her eyes full of helpless tears, she carefully straightened and took a firmer grip on the hedge. 'Let me go. I can manage by myself.'

'Please yourself.' His mouth twisting derisively, he released her so abruptly that she toppled backwards and slid down on to her bottom, an expression of surprised fury on her face.

'You bastard!' she yelled furiously. 'You rotten, lousy, smug, sanctimonious bastard!'

'Ah, that's better,' he sneered, 'the Miss Markham we all know and love.' Leaning down, he hauled her unceremoniously to her feet and propped her against the hedge as though she were a shop-window dummy he didn't know what else to do with.

'I hate you,' she gritted tearfully as she pushed her sopping hair off her face. 'Do you know that? I really hate you!'

'Yes, because I'm the one man who can see through your act! So what's it to be? Inside? Or back to your car? Because I'm not standing about out here getting soaked to the skin!'

'Who asked you to?' God, it was ridiculous. She leaning in a wet hedge, the rain lashing down like fury soaking her to her underwear, her ankle screaming with pain, and the pair of them arguing in the pitch dark in the middle of nowhere.

'Well?' he demanded impatiently as he raked back his own dripping hair. 'What's it to be?'

Glaring at him, wanting to tell him to go to hell and knowing the stupidity of doing any such thing, she muttered, 'Inside.'

Transferring her grip to his sweater as he steadied her, she hopped round to face the cottage.

'Oh, this is ridiculous!' he complained as he nearly lost his own footing on the muddy path. With a grunt of effort he swung her off her feet and into his arms and before she could do more than squeal he was kicking open the unlatched front door and striding into the lounge. Dumping her without ceremony into the armchair, he stood hands on hips staring down at her. 'Thank you,' he prompted sarcastically.

'Thank you,' she gritted.

With a look of dislike, he turned away and went out, slamming the door behind him.

'And the same to you,' she whispered shakily. Leaning carefully back, she gripped the arms of the chair in an effort to overcome the pain that sent every other thought out of her head. Gradually, as she took controlled, shallow breaths, the white-hot agony settled to a dull throbbing and she slowly allowed her tensed muscles to relax. Turning her head, she stared about her at the small shabby room. There didn't seem to be any personal touches, not even a book that she could see, just a spartan, functional room. Hearing a muffled slam, she stiffened warily. Her eyes fixed on the door, she only relaxed when she heard a car start up followed by the angry revving of a powerful engine. Where the hell was he going? The local pub? Without warning, tears of self-pity welled into her eyes and she sniffed, turning her head to stare at the fire. It wasn't fair. And how the hell was she to get back to London when she couldn't drive? And what was Thelma going to think? She'd be worried sick. What she needed was a phone. Staring round her, not seeing one, she slid down on to her knees and began to crawl out to the hall, her bad foot carefully raised. She should never have come, she thought defeatedly. Had she really expected that he would listen to her? Understand? Yes, she had, because she thought that, once he'd had a chance to think about it, he would realise that she couldn't have been entirely to blame. Only he obviously hadn't realised any such thing.

Finding no phone in the hall, she crawled into the kitchen. Nothing. Retracing her route, she pulled herself back into the chair and, with a long shaky sigh, she carefully eased her bad leg over the other one, leaned her head back into the corner and closed her eyes. Now what? And where the hell was Mackenzie? He surely hadn't abandoned her? Oh, no? she thought derisively. Glancing at her watch, she saw that it was, surprisingly, nearly eight o'clock. Where had the time gone? And she was hungry, she suddenly realised. She'd had no lunch, no dinner. . .

Picking irritably at a hole in the chair arm, she brooded on her ill usage. She was soaking wet, in pain, hungry, thirsty—and every damned time she met Mackenzie something went wrong. It had been raining the day she'd driven him to Yorkshire, and that cottage had been small and spartan. Fate? she wondered sleepily. Certainly it had had the same damned uncomfortable sleeping arrangements!

Closing her eyes, intending to only rest for a moment, she fell asleep. Even the pain in her foot didn't keep her awake, nor Mackenzie returning some hours later to cover her with a blanket. Snuggling more comfortably into the chair, she slept till morning and it wasn't until small, unfamiliar sounds intruded that she stirred and slowly opened her eyes. A soft wool blanket covered her and she frowned down at it for a moment before looking up. Without moving, she stared at the hunched shape of Mackenzie as he raked out the ashes from the fire and relaid it with new kindling. He'd obviously washed and shaved, and his dark hair had been tidily combed. He was dressed in a navy V-necked sweater over a pale blue shirt, his long legs encased in jeans that were pulled tight across his powerful thighs. His face was intent, unaware of her observation; a bleak face—and she gave a faint, unconscious sigh that inadvertently alerted him. She saw him stiffen slightly before he slowly turned his head, and she wished she'd remained sleeping. He looked as unyielding as he had the night before.

Easing herself stiffly upright, she dragged her breath in sharply as her injured foot touched the floor. Her breath held, her eyes tight shut, she waited for the pain to subside.

'I take it this theatrical performance means your foot is no better?' he asked coldly, not an atom of compassion in his voice.

Opening her eyes, she shook her head, and tears glistened on her lashes for a moment before she blinked them away.

Sighly loudly, he leaned towards her and she flinched away. 'For God's sake!' he exploded. 'What do you think I'm going to do?'

'Sorry,' she mumbled.

'Grit your teeth,' he instructed impatiently as he grasped her foot in surprisingly gentle hands and rested it on his knee.

'I am,' she gasped, but was unable to stop the yelp of pain as he quickly and efficiently tugged her boot free. White and shaking, she clutched frantically at the chair arms as wave after wave of pain washed over her, bringing beads of perspiration to her forehead. 'Oh, God.' When the pain eventually settled back to a dull throbbing, she eased her breath out, slowly opened her eyes and stared in disbelief at her rapidly swelling ankle. Without the boot's restriction, the flesh seemed to be slowly inflating, like a balloon. It wasn't until she heard Mackenzie's indrawn hiss of breath that she looked up. Just for a second, he looked concerned, compassionate, but then the mask was back in place and she wondered if she'd imagined it.

'Tights or stockings?' he demanded peremptorily.

'What?'

'Are you wearing tights or stockings?' he repeated impatiently.

'Oh, stockings.'

'Then take it off!'

With a little glare, she discreetly unhooked her stocking and rolled it down.

With a sound of exasperation, and without warning,

he whisked it from her foot, and the relief was enormous as, unrestricted, the swollen flesh released its grip on the nerve-endings that had been causing such pain.

'It will have to be X-rayed,' he said without looking up.

'Yes,' she agreed weakly.

'In fact, it should have been X-rayed last night,' he added angrily.

Staring at him in disbelief, she retorted, 'Quite possibly, only it would have taken more courage than I possessed to insist you take me to the hospital!'

'Don't be bloody stupid!' Dragging the small coffee-table across, he carefully rested her foot on it before getting to his feet. 'I'll make some tea.'

Staring after him as he went out, she pursed her lips in disgust. What the hell was that supposed to mean? Stupid for not telling him? Or stupid for not believing he'd have helped? Shaking her head, she eased herself into a more comfortable position and only then remembered that Thelma didn't know what the hell had happened to her. 'Mackenzie?' she called.

'What?' he asked moodily.

'I have to telephone Thelma—she'll be worried sick! I should have rung her last night.'

'You can ring her from the hospital,' he said indifferently.

'And where were you last night?' she shouted after him. 'Leaving me here on my own. . .'

'You really expected me to stay here with you?' he asked incredulously as he came to stand in the doorway. 'You think I haven't learned anything?'

'Well, of all the. . .'

'All the what?' he demanded. 'You really think I'm stupid enough to give you more ammunition?' With a look that might have stripped paint, he went back to the kitchen and she heard him banging cups and saucers about in temper.

When he returned, carrying two mugs of tea, she

watched him with a sour expression. So confident, she thought mutinously. So sure he was always right. Absently accepting the mug he handed her, she continued to watch him until he raised one eyebrow in query, a haughty little gesture that infuriated her. Sipping the hot liquid, feeling the warmth explore her stomach, she wondered whether there was even any point in trying to make him understand.

'I am sorry,' she said quietly as though the previous evening's conversation hadn't been interrupted. 'About your business and everything.' Looking up at him, her eyes serious and intent, she added, 'It truly wasn't done to be malicious or cause trouble.'

With a look of disbelief, he leaned his broad shoulders against the mantelshelf, his mug held between his palms; a tall, brooding figure that made her feel lost and rather insignificant.

'Will you at least try to look at it from my point of view?' she persevered.

'Nothing you can say, or explain, will make one iota of difference to my feelings for you,' he said dismissively.

'I know! That wasn't what I meant!' she insisted. 'I wasn't trying to justify my behaviour, just explain how I could have been so stupid.'

'Not stupid,' he contradicted flatly, 'criminal, and if this refusal to give in to feminine vanity by not combing your hair or cleaning your face is intended to impress me, it doesn't,' he concluded nastily.

'What the hell has my appearance got to do with anything?' she asked in exasperation. 'It's completely irrelevant! Anyway I don't have a comb. I don't have anything, and even if I did, and I combed my hair, no doubt that would also have brought forth a censorious comment on trying to impress you by titivating!' Giving him a look of irritation, she tried again. 'I know your opinion of me isn't likely to change. You're too damned convinced of your own invincibility for that to happen, but I did hope that you could set aside your prejudices long enough to at least let me know how Daniel was. What the hell difference can it make if you tell me? I'm not likely to meet him, or corrupt his judgement, as you obviously seem to consider!'

'You think I should forgive and forget?'

'No,' she denied on a long sigh, 'and, to be honest, I don't know that I would be able to do so if the roles were reversed, but I hope I would have the decency to find out the facts before jumping to conclusions——'

'Decency?' he exploded, making her jump. 'Lord, but you've got a nerve! You attempt to destroy my reputation, do possibly untold harm to my son, and then have the gall to expect me to be decent!' Thumping his mug down on the mantelpiece, he strode the short distance to her and, bending down, his face thrust close against hers, grated, 'You come trundling up here with your little-girl air of contrition and expect me to understand! That I will immediately launch into a friendly tale of how my son is coping!'

'I didn't——'

'Shut up!' he snarled. Leaning closer so that Neile was forced to press herself into the cushions to get away from him, he continued savagely, 'You schemed and plotted behind my back to get my son away from me into the clutches of that—that psychopath!' he burst out, clearly unable to think of a suitable epiphet to describe his ex-wife. 'And then calmly expect me to tell you how he is!'

'No!' she shouted. Feeling claustrophobic with his bulk looming over her, she thumped her fists impotently against his chest. Not even sure if it was to try and move him, or out of frustration, she continued bitterly, 'I didn't plot anything! How the hell was I supposed to know what she was like? Or you, for that matter? You didn't exactly go out of your way to be pleasant to me! And I only denigrated your character to her when it became obvious what she was trying to do. I didn't know she was going to twist it all round, did I?'

'Yes, you bloody well did! I told you what she was like. Told you I had to be careful.'

'I was careful!'

'You were what?' he exclaimed with a look of astonishment. 'You deliberately and maliciously set out to ensure that Daniel was sent back to her!'

'I did not!' Shoving him away, she was quite unprepared for him to grab her arms and haul her up out of the chair and hold her tight in front of him. 'Let me go! You're hurting my foot!'

'I'm not touching your foot! Do you deny she came to your office?'

'Of course I don't deny it!'

'There you are, then!'

'It isn't "there you are, then" at all!' she retorted, incensed. 'She took me by surprise!'

'Then why say anything at all?'

'Because she took me by surprise!' she shouted. 'Because she's a clever little bitch and I'm stupid!' Staring up into his harsh, angry face that was so close that she could see the dark flecks in his silvery eyes, see every dark lash fringing them, she only gradually became aware of the feel of his hard body pressed against hers, and she wriggled to be free. 'Let go of me!'

'Why? Bother you, does it?' he asked nastily.

'No, it doesn't bother me!'

'Well, it bothers me,' he stated unexpectedly, his mouth twisted in self-contempt.

Her eyes widening in astonishment, then fear, she attempted to wrench herself away. 'Don't you dare touch me,' she whispered, her throat dry and aching.

'Dare, Neile? Dare?' he queried with soft menace.

Feeling almost suffocated by the expression in his eyes, which were fixed on her with almost hypnotic intensity, she shook her head in mute denial, and knew exactly what was going to happen a split second before it did. 'No,' she managed before his mouth touched hers.

It burned, she thought hazily, seemed to fuse against

hers, and she drew in a sharp, shocked breath before trying to struggle free.

'Cold and passionless?' he growled against her mouth. 'Isn't that what you said?'

'No,' she breathed, 'please don't do this. . .'

'Why?' Crushing her slim frame almost brutally against him, he returned his mouth to hers.

Clutching frantically at his sweater to maintain her balance, shaken by an overwhelming desire to respond, she tried to clamp her lips tight together, only to be defeated by his superior strength as teeth and tongue rasped against hers, almost brutally forcing her mouth wider. Groaning with pain and fear at what this man could do to her, how he could so easily arouse feelings she didn't want aroused, she moved her hands to his neck and tried to force him away only to find that the feel of his warm flesh beneath her fingers robbed her of will.

Shuddering, she finally managed to drag her mouth free and bury her hot face in his neck. Oh, God, how could she be so aware of a man who hated her? A man she wasn't sure she even liked any more? The warmth of his arousal was tight against her and she drew in shuddery little breaths as she tried to ignore it. Only Mackenzie wasn't a man to be ignored easily. His palms were warm against her back where they had roved beneath her sweater without her even noticing, his mouth was against her hair and she clutched him tighter, not wanting to lift her face to the merciless regard she was sure she would see.

'Bitch,' he muttered raggedly as his hands unconsciously massaged the warm flesh of her back.

Her own arms clamped tight around him, she remained mute. Anything she said was likely to exacerbate an already explosive situation. She could feel the tension in him, the anger and the pain, so she stayed quiet, breath held.

'Is that what you wanted, Neile?' he grated, his voice not quite steady. 'Why you came?'

Mortified he should think so, she gave a frantic shake of her head and burrowed closer against his solid frame. But wasn't it? a little voice asked inside her head. Wasn't it what you always wanted? From the first time you met him? Why you said those things to Caroline? Because he only casually mentioned that he might get in touch with you, in six months? A year? Because you were piqued? No! 'No,' she whispered, more as a denial to herself than to him.

One hand moving to her hair, he brutally pulled her head back so that he could look down into her face. 'Wide, innocent eyes,' he said softly, 'eyes of a temptress.' As he pushed her away his mouth twisted contemptuously, but whether for his own actions, or hers, she didn't know. Maybe a bit of both.

She searched his face, as he was searching hers, and gave a helpless sigh. 'I don't know,' she admitted honestly. Trying to seek out her own truth, her own motives, she repeated helplessly, 'I truly don't know. Not consciously, not maliciously.' Pushing her tumbled hair back with a tired hand, she tried to collect her thoughts. 'When Caroline came to the office looking small and beautiful and helpless, I was taken off guard,' she explained simply. 'She was the last person I expected to come through my door. She told me she loved you. . . She did!' she insisted when he gave a disbelieving grunt. 'She said she wanted you back. And when I said—oh, I don't know, something about I wasn't stopping you, that I barely knew you, she said that staying the night together in an isolated cottage hardly sounded as though we were mere acquaintances. Oh, Mackenzie, she sounded so damned plausible! Her little-girl voice, her eyes misted with tears. . .'

'And then?' he asked flatly.

'And then—well, I couldn't deny it, could I?' she asked despairingly.

'Of course you could have denied it!'

'Not when I didn't know what she wanted! Why she was asking me! And then I noticed that the man with her was writing it all down and I realised too late that I'd fallen right into the hole she'd dug, and that was when I tried to backtrack, protect you by saying those other things. . .'

'God give me strength. A child would have known what she was up to! Oh, no, Neile, that won't wash. If you had really been trying to protect me, you'd have said nothing. . .'

'Do you think I don't wish I had?' she asked bitterly.

'No,' he refuted flatly. 'I don't. I think you made a calculated decision and the words you used were well thought out in advance——'

'How could they be thought out in advance?' she demanded. 'I didn't know she was coming. . .' Breaking off, her brows drawn into a frown, she stared at him blindly before asking faintly, 'But how on earth did she know where I was? Who I was, even? Do you know, I never even considered that? I was so angry with myself for being stupid that it never occurred to me how she knew who I was or where I worked. You obviously didn't tell her, so who did?'

Giving her a look of disgust, he asked wearily, 'What the hell does it matter?'

'Well, of course it matters!' she insisted urgently. 'She knew, Mackenzie! She knew!' Still staring at him, she suddenly jabbed a finger in his chest. 'How did she know about the cottage? Hmm? Tell me that!'

'Oh, for goodness' sake! She knew about the cottage because you told her!'

'But I didn't!'

'You must have done!'

'No,' she insisted. 'I didn't.' Her eyes screwed up in concentration, she thought back to that day. 'She said——'

'Neile,' he cut in impatiently, 'It——'

'No, wait,' she insisted, flapping her hand at him to shut him up. 'She came into the office and she said she'd come to thank me, said something about she hoped I hadn't taken your advances seriously, or something like that,' she said quickly as he tried to interrupt again. 'I said you hadn't made any, that everything had been perfectly innocent, and she said hardly innocent when you spent the night in an isolated cottage!' she finished triumphantly. 'She knew!' Pinching her bottom lip thoughtfully between her finger and thumb, she continued slowly, 'She definitely knew. But how? That's what we need to find out. . .'

'No, it isn't! What the hell difference does it make now? The damage has been done!'

'Yes! But not by me! And I want to know how she found out,' she declared angrily, 'even if for my own damned satisfaction. Do you think I'd have been so concerned about Daniel, followed you, if I'd deliberately set out to hurt you? I barely knew you; why on earth would I want to hurt you?'

'How the hell should I know? It's all part of the damned game women play, isn't it?'

'No! How can you say that?'

'Easily,' he bit out irritably.

Easily? she wondered. Because he knew so many woman? Because he'd cheated on Caroline before? And, when she'd found out, had she played games to get him back? Frowning in thought, she continued to stare at him. Driven by Mars, Ellen had said. Ariens had a passionate nature! Jealous and possessive. . .

'Now what are you scheming?'

'I'm not scheming anything!' she denied forcefully.

With a grunt that sounded suspiciously like disbelief, and an abrupt movement that she knew wasn't intentional, he pushed her away so that she overbalanced and fell backwards into the chair.

With a screech of agony as her bad foot jarred against the floor, she hunched over, holding her leg with both hands until the nausea passed. Taking a deep, shaky breath, she stared up at him, her face white.

'I'm sorry,' he apologised awkwardly. Sounding incredibly weary and fed up with the whole thing, he added dismissively, 'Maybe you were hoping to get something out of it.'

'Like what? We're not all money-grubbing opportunists, you know, and I certainly didn't need your cash.'

'Yes, you did.'

'What?' she asked blankly, and then felt an icy finger slide down her spine at the expression on his face.

'I said, yes, you did. Didn't you? The agency wasn't doing very well, was it?'

'No,' she agreed quietly. 'You knew that; I told you when we were in Yorkshire.'

'Yes. And then, suddenly, it started to pick up, didn't it?'

'We did some advertising. . . How do you know?' she whispered.

'Because I asked around.'

Staring at him, her eyes narrowed, she asked quietly, 'Just what are you trying to say, Mackenzie?'

'Merely that when you were on the verge of folding a sudden injection of cash obviously saved you. How else could you afford to advertise?'

'That was a bank loan!'

'Was it?'

'Yes. I'd hardly lie about something that could be proved by a quick call to my bank manager, would I?'

'Wouldn't you?'

'No! That was why you had me investigated? To see if, or how much, Caroline had paid me?'

'Partly,' he admitted.

'And the other reason?'

'I was going to ruin you,' he stated flatly, his eyes holding hers. 'I was going to punish you, make you pay, as you'd made me pay.'

'But you didn't,' she whispered, her throat dry. 'Or

NO RISK, NO OBLIGATION TO BUY...NOW OR EVER!

GUARANTEED

PLAY "ROLL A DOUBLE" AND GET AS MANY AS FIVE FREE GIFTS!

HERE'S HOW TO PLAY:

1. Peel off label from front cover. Place it in space provided at right. With a coin, carefully scratch off the silver dice. This makes you eligible to receive two or more free books, and possibly another gift, depending on what is revealed beneath the scratch-off area.

2. You'll receive brand-new Harlequin Presents® novels. When you return this card, we'll rush you the books and gift you qualify for ABSOLUTELY FREE!

3. Then, if we don't hear from you, every month we'll send you 6 additional novels to read and enjoy months before they arrive in stores. You can return them and owe nothing, but if you decide to keep them, you'll pay only $2.49* per book— a saving of 40¢ each off the cover price.

4. When you subscribe to the Harlequin Reader Service®, you'll also get our subscribers'-only newsletter, as well as additional free gifts from time to time.

5. You must be completely satisfied. You may cancel at any time simply by sending us a note or a shipping statement marked "cancel" or by returning any shipment to us at our expense.

The Austrian crystal sparkles like a diamond! And it's carefully set in a romantic ''Key to Your Heart'' pendant on a generous 18″ gold-tone chain. The entire necklace is yours free as added thanks for giving our Reader Service a try!

HARLEQUIN "NO RISK" GUARANTEE

- You're not required to buy a single book—ever!
- You must be completely satisfied or you may cancel at any time simply by sending us a note or shipping statement marked "cancel" or by returning any shipment to us at our cost. Either way, you will receive no more books; you'll have no obligation to buy.
- The free books and gift you claimed on this "Roll A Double" offer remain yours to keep no matter what you decide.

If offer card is missing, please write to: Harlequin Reader Service, 3010 Walden Ave., P.O. Box 1867, Buffalo, NY 14269-1867 haven't yet,' she added as she remembered that he had been in the States and therefore probably hadn't had time. Licking dry lips, she asked weakly, 'Are you still going to?'

With a little shrug, he turned away and stared down at the fire. With seeming idleness, he lifted one foot and pushed a log back into place before returning his gaze to her. 'On the other hand, you probably aren't worth the bother. Anyway,' he added impatiently, 'it has nothing to do with the farradiddle you're spouting now.'

'It's not a farradiddle,' she denied automatically. 'She knew, and I intend to find out how.'

'And how are you going to do that?' he asked derisively. 'Go and ask her?'

'No,' she denied, her brows still drawn in a frown as she continued to speculate. 'We must have been followed,' she decided, speaking her thoughts out loud, and when he made a sound of disgust she glared at him defiantly. 'Well, how else would she know?'

'How the hell could anyone have followed us?' he demanded. 'We didn't even know where we were!'

'That doesn't mean we couldn't have been followed,' she persisted.

'By whom?'

'I don't know, do I? Yes, I do!' she suddenly declared, her eyes widening as she suddenly remembered a little incident that had puzzled her. 'The fair man!' Focusing on his face, which was wearing a pitying expression, her mouth tightened crossly. 'When you took Daniel inside the house, I got out to stretch my legs and I saw a tall, fair-haired man duck out of sight when he saw me watching. I saw him again in the pub when we went to have something to eat. He could have followed us.'

'Oh, sure. Sat in his car all night to keep the cottage under observation. Followed us to the garage, down the motorway, and then of course he would have had to follow you up to town the next day. Do talk sense, Neile!'

'He could have done,' she insisted lamely. 'How else could she have known?'

'I don't know,' he denied irritably, 'and am now beginning to wonder if I very much care! Did you see any signs of a car following us when we were lost? Well, did you?'

'No,' she admitted grumpily.

'There you are, then.'

Pulling a face of disgust, she threw herself backwards in her chair and accidentally jarred her foot. Whimpering in pain, she hunched over and hugged herself in an effort to minimise it.

Clicking his tongue in annoyance presumably, he righted the coffee-table, plonked the cushion on it, then gently replaced her foot. Seeing the mug he had given her earlier upended on the floor, a spreading stain on the rug from the contents, he picked that up as well and stood it in the hearth before returning his attention to Neile. Waiting patiently until she'd regained control, he agreed wearily, 'All right, all right, if you didn't tell her, then someone else obviously did.'

'Thank you,' she retorted tartly.

'Don't be sarcastic,' he reproved fairly mildly. 'Now start from the beginning—and if you're lying, Neile, God help you.'

CHAPTER SIX

WHEN Neile had finished, going over some points twice in an effort to remember everything Caroline had said or insinuated, and her own answers, Mackenzie exploded disgustedly, 'Then why in God's name didn't you tell me that in the first place?'

'Because you wouldn't listen!' she exclaimed in astonishment. 'Every time I opened my mouth, you told me to shut up!'

With a crochety shrug, he muttered awkwardly, 'Well, there's nothing much we can do at the moment; it's all water under the bridge—and you have to have that foot X-rayed.'

'And that's it?' she asked incredulously. 'You're just going to leave it there?'

'No, I'm not just going to leave it there,' he denied irritably. Turning on his heel, he walked out and returned a few seconds later carrying a leather holdall which he dumped on the floor.

'Are you going somewhere?' she asked lamely.

'What?' Following the direction of her gaze towards his bag, he gave her a look of derision. 'Of course I'm going somewhere. I'm going home.'

'Home?' she echoed stupidly. 'Don't you live here?'

'Of course I don't live here,' he retorted dismissively. 'I mean, is it likely? From what you know of me, is it likely that I'd live in this hovel?'

'Well, I don't know, do I? You said. . .' Shutting her mouth with a snap and giving him a look of disgust she struggled upright. 'Is there a bathroom I can use?'

'Upstairs,' he answered with horrible mockery. 'Can you manage?'

'Do I look as though I can?' she demanded waspishly.

With a twisted smile, he walked across to her, swept her up into his arms and carried her to the foot of the stairs.

'I can manage from here,' she insisted quickly. 'I can go up on my bottom.' Even if their proximity wasn't having any effect on him, it was on her, but the speed with which he complied with her request was hardly flattering, she decided miserably as he dumped her with no more concern than he'd shown the previous evening.

Levering herself upwards, she then hopped along to the antiquated bathroom. Perching on the edge of the bath, she leaned her face on the cool porcelain of the sink for a moment to get her breath back, and also needing the moment alone to think, sort out the muddle in her mind. Remembering back to the first time she'd met him, she tried to recall what her initial reaction had been, if she had been so conscious of his nearness. She'd been wary of him, she remembered, afraid of the tug of attraction she'd felt—and why the hell wasn't he going to do anything about what she'd told him? she wondered irritably as her mind went off at a tangent.

Feeling tired and crotchety, she slammed the plug in the sink before running cold water into it. Well, one thing was for sure, even if Mackenzie wasn't going to do anything about it, she intended to. She had every intention of trying to find out how Caroline had known about the cottage and where she'd worked.

Absently dabbling her fingers in the cold water, she stared at the wall as she tried to remember every detail of her meeting with the other woman. Everything that had happened before she'd walked agitatedly across to the window. . . Jerking upright, she stared at herself in the spotted mirror, her expression startled. Stupid, stupid, stupid, she castigated herself. That same fair man who she'd seen in Yorkshire had been leaning casually against Caroline's car. She'd even seen him grin and say something to her before helping her into it.

She'd been so bewildered at the time that it just hadn't registered.

Forgetting her bad foot, she leapt to her feet, then gave a scream of pain as her ankle gave way beneath her. Clutching the sink for support, she dragged deep breaths into her lungs in an effort to stop herself passing out, then nearly fell again as Mackenzie came bursting through the door and skidded to a halt on the worn lino.

'What?' he demanded.

Unable to answer for a moment, she stayed still, head bowed over the sink until strong arms encircled her and gently turned her round. His glance raking her pasty face, he clicked his tongue, which could have indicated anything from disgust to compassion, before lowering her to sit on the bathroom stool. Pulling off a handful of toilet paper, he damped it in the sink before gently grasping her chin and sponging her face.

'All right now?'

Nodding, she gave him a shaky smile. 'Yes, sorry, I forgot and jumped up. Mackenzie? You know that fair man I told you about? Well, he was waiting outside my office for Caroline that day——'

'Oh Neile, can't you just leave it?'

Shaking her head, her eyes fixed on his, she whispered, 'I have to know. I'm not lying, Mackenzie, not making it up, and I can't forgive myself for my stupidity.'

'And you need to find a reason to exonerate yourself?' he asked surprisingly gently.

'Yes. And, if we can find out the truth, you could maybe get Daniel back.'

'I already have Daniel,' he told her quietly.

'What?' she queried blankly. 'But you said——'

'I know what I said.' Sighing, he perched on the edge of the bath and stared at her for several moments before explaining quietly, 'We agreed on a settlement figure, and Daniel was given into my custody.'

'But you went to the States on your own. . .'

'No, Daniel had already gone out on an earlier flight.'

'I see. I'm glad. Is he all right?'

'Yes. Now, this fair man—describe him to me.'

Trying to picture the man in her mind, she began slowly, 'He was tall, about your height I'd guess, only thinner, quite a lot thinner. The first time I saw him he was wearing dark trousers and one of those army sweaters—you know, with the leather elbow and shoulder patches. The same in the pub. Rather a narrow, bony face, sort of aquiline nose and soft fair hair that fell over his forehead.' Unaware of Mackenzie's arrested expression, she continued thoughtfully, 'When I saw him outside the office, he was wearing a grey suit. . . He was,' she insisted when Mackenzie made a flat denial.

Waving his hand as though to deny what he'd said, he got to his feet, his face closed. 'If you're lying, Neile. . .Oh, never mind. Can you manage?'

Nodding, she watched as he walked out and quietly closed the door. Did he know the man? Was that why he'd said no? Not because he didn't believe her, but because he didn't believe it could be who he thought it was? And, if he did know him, was that why he didn't want to do anything about it? Oh, hell, instead of becoming clearer, everything seemed to get more and more complicated. With a long sigh of her own, she picked up the dampened tissue he'd used and carefully wiped away her smudged mascara. Running her tongue round her teeth and grimacing in disgust, she dragged her fingers through her tangled hair. What a mess. She looked like the Wreck of the Hesperus. With a defeated sigh, she got awkwardly up. Using the bathroom wall for balance, she hopped out then along the landing to the stairs and went down them the same way she'd gone up.

Mackenzie was waiting for her and, the moment she reached the bottom, he helped her upright then steadied her as she balanced on one foot, and she found it took enormous strength of will not to lean against him, seek comfort.

'I've put your boot and stocking in the car,' he said abruptly, effectively shattering any ideas she might have had that he was softening towards her. 'Anything else?'

'No,' she denied quietly. She didn't have anything else, except Thelma's car keys.

'I've also put your car in the garage; it should be safe enough until it can be collected.' His expression was as uninterested as his voice. Too uninterested? she wondered with a faint twinge of hope. Then hastily abandoned that line of thought. That was like building sandcastles in a gale. Allowing herself to be swung up into his arms, she rested her head against him as he carried her out to the car.

Thoroughly despondent, and not wanting him to see how miserable she was feeling, she kept her lashes lowered. The hard jaw so close to her hand invited touch and she had to clench her fingers to stay them.

'Open the car door, will you?'

Leaning down, she did so, then pulled herself awkwardly on to the seat. He'd folded a blanket on the floor for her injured foot and she thanked him quietly. Keeping her gaze fixed resolutely through the windscreen, she stared out over the long gleaming bonnet. Uncomfortably aware of every movement he made as he climbed behind the wheel, she wished she could ignore the warm feel of his arm against hers, the male scent of him. Still feeling slightly sick, she clipped her seatbelt in place and closed her eyes.

It didn't take more than half an hour to drive to the hospital and fortunately the casualty department was nearly empty. As Mackenzie helped her through the doors, there was a sudden flurry of activity as a porter and a male nurse rushed to offer her assistance. Their jocular rivalry would have been hysterically funny if she hadn't caught a glimpse of Mackenzie's face. If looks could have killed, all three of them would have been lying dead.

His abrupt withdrawal from the proceedings made his

feelings more than clear; his harsh words really weren't necessary. 'My God, just can't wait, can they?' he observed disgustedly. 'Give me Thelma's number—I'll go and phone her while you're being seen to.'

One either side of her, the two men helped her to one of the cubicles, and, with a broad wink, the young nurse drew the curtain across. Sighing for the futility of it all, she sat on the bed and waited.

When she returned to the waiting-room over an hour later, pushed in a creaky wheelchair, her injured foot outstretched, Mackenzie swung round from the window where he had been staring morosely out. 'Not broken, then,' he commented as he stared at her bandaged foot.

'No, and you don't need to sound as though you thought I were some sort of hypochondriac and had made the whole thing up,' she retorted petulantly.

'So what is wrong with it?'

'Bad sprain,' the porter, elderly this time, told him laconically. 'Torn muscle, very painful. She's not to walk on it,' he instructed as though he expected Mackenzie to immediately order her to her feet.

'I'm fine,' she interrupted hastily before Mackenzie could say something rude, which he looked quite capable of doing.

'You don't look it,' he grumbled. 'You look like a bloody ghost.' Standing at the foot of her chair, he stared into her white face, which had the effect of making her feel even more ghost-like. Her foot throbbed dully, like toothache, and she felt like crying. Not gently, but sobbing like a baby. Wincing as the porter swung her chair too fast, she looked helplessly at Mackenzie as the porter waited expectantly for him to open the door.

'Miserable sod,' he muttered as he did so. Walking ahead, he opened the car door and helped her in. Dismissing the porter with a curt nod, he climbed behind the wheel. 'What happened to the two stooges—break their hearts already, did you?'

'Oh, stop it, Mackenzie,' she exclaimed wearily, 'it was only a bit of harmless fun.'

Slamming his seatbelt into the slot, he observed moodily, 'Yeah, harmless, it always is. Did they give you something for the pain?'

'Yes, some tablets,' she explained and showed him the little bottle before putting it on the parcel shelf in front of her.

'How long before you can walk on it?'

'A few weeks.' She sighed as she envisaged all sorts of problems, not least of which was how she was supposed to get up three flights of rickety stairs to her office. And the doctor's instruction to stay off the injured foot was ridiculous. She couldn't take a month off work. Maybe she could get some crutches from her local hospital. Turning her head, she stared listlessly out of the window and only gradually registered the open fields. Frowning, she asked in puzzlement, 'Isn't the station in the town?'

'Station?' he queried as he flicked her a curious glance. 'Why on earth do you want to know about stations?'

Sorely tempted to tell him she was an avid train-spotter, she snapped. 'So that I can get a train! They do go from stations, you know!'

'I know very well where they go from! It's what you want one for that I was trying to elicit. And your damned sarcasm I can well do without!'

'Sorry,' she mumbled grudgingly, then added pathetically, 'My foot hurts.' Taking a deep breath, she continued more quietly, 'As I'm unable to drive, I assumed you were taking me to the station when we left the hospital so that I could get a train back to London.'

'Then you assumed wrong. You're staying with me until I get this whole mess sorted out.'

Turning towards him, she stared at his set face in shock. Stay with him? Oh, no. No way. 'Don't be ridiculous! I couldn't possibly stay with you. I don't even have so much as a toothbrush. I'm sorry, but I have to go back to London.'

'It wasn't an invitation, Neile,' he said softly. 'It was an order.'

'Well, order or not, I can't stay with you. I'm very glad that you're going to sort everything out, but you don't need me for that. Besides I have to be back at work as soon as possible.'

'Tough,' he said unsympathetically, 'and I dare say even you aren't indispensable—let Thelma get a temp in. Anyway, you can't go back to work with that foot.'

'Then I'll stay in my flat.'

'You'll stay with me,' he put in flatly. 'Besides which, I need you to identify the fair man. Don't I? Don't I, Neile?' he insisted softly when she refused to answer.

'I don't want to stay with you,' she muttered childishly. 'I want to go home.'

'Well, you can't. Go to sleep or something.'

Turning her head away, she felt tears prick behind her eyes. She didn't want to stay with him. How could she? They'd done nothing but argue and shout at each other for the past twenty-four hours—well, almost, she qualified to herself, but what on earth would they be like after a few days? Assuming it was only for a few days, and she didn't think she could cope for much longer with his constant proximity. She didn't feel very well either, she suddenly realised. She felt hot and clammy and shivery. Perhaps it was the pills the doctor had given her; he'd made her take two before she left the hospital. Perhaps they didn't agree with her. But if she was going to be ill she wanted to be at home, not with him, not in a strange house. Leaning her hot forehead against the cool glass of the window, she closed her eyes, then snapped them quickly open when the world revolved sickeningly. 'Mackenzie,' she whispered tragically, 'I don't feel very well.'

'Oh, lord,' he muttered wearily. Swerving off the road on to the grass verge, he hauled on the handbrake and turned towards her. Feeling her hot forehead, he made an exasperated sound in the back of his throat. 'You're burning up.'

'I know,' she agreed unhappily.

'Feel sick?'

'A bit; perhaps if I were to have the window open, take deep breaths. . .'

Pressing a switch on the console, he opened the window and Neile took deep gulps of the cold air. 'Do you want to lie in the back?'

'No, I'll be all right, I expect. Perhaps it was the pain-killers I took.'

'Perhaps,' he agreed, but he didn't sound totally convinced. 'Well, we'll be home in half an hour or so, so you can lie down then; only if you begin to feel sick for God's sake say so and I'll stop the car!'

'All right.' He was probably terrified she'd be sick all over his upholstery. With a pathetic sniff, she held her face to the cool breeze as he drew back on to the road. 'I don't want to be ill,' she whispered, more to herself than to her companion. 'I hate being ill.'

'Well, just hang on till we get home,' he encouraged helplessly.

Glancing at him, seeing the lines of worry creasing his forehead, she suddenly realised that he didn't have a clue what to do. Like most men, illness obviously horrified him, especially unidentified illness, and he hadn't a clue what to do for the best. Giving him a small, reassuring smile, which in the circumstances was ludicrous, she said comfortingly, 'I'll be all right; maybe it's hunger.'

'Hunger?' he exclaimed in astonishment as though he'd never in his life heard of anyone feeling unwell from hunger. 'When did you last eat?'

'I don't know—breakfast yesterday, I think. I had some cereal before I went to work.'

'Well, there you are, then,' he pronounced in relief as though that quite satisfactorily disposed of the subject of her illness, 'it's probably hunger.'

As she stared at him, a reluctant smile danced in her eyes. Oh, Mackenzie, she thought, you really are a sod sometimes. Leaning her head back, she concentrated on taking deep breaths, her eyes fixed on the mascot on the front of the bonnet, and within a few minutes he'd pulled off the main road into a tree-lined avenue. She hadn't a clue where they were, and even if she asked him the answer wasn't likely to be enlightening. She didn't know this area at all, but hopefully they were nearly at their destination. It looked a very bleak sort of place, a bit like Yorkshire; long, rolling hills covered in mist, valleys, rocky outcrops, a few scattered sheep. Nothing very much to take her mind off her troubles, and she let her mind wander and suddenly remembered that he never had told her whose house it was she'd spent the night in.

'Whose house was it? Where we've just been?'

'It belongs to an American client. It was left to him in his great-aunt's will and he asked me to look it over when I got back to the UK. I was supposed to have had a meeting with an estate agent there today!' he added in obvious indignation.

'Oh,' she said lamely.

'Yes, oh. It was damned inconvenient having to ring him and put him off.'

'Sorry. So where did you spend the night if you didn't spend it there?'

'In the local pub!'

'Oh,' she said again, losing interest. Giving him a speculative look, she added, 'If you couldn't trust your reputation at the house, how come you can trust it in your home?'

'Because I have a housekeeper! And I wouldn't be taking you there at all if I could avoid it, believe me. Only I can't avoid it, can I? I need you to identify someone.'

'The fair man,' she stated with a little nod. 'Who is he?'

'That's what we are about to find out. From your description, he sounds very much like my chauffeur.'

'Your chauffeur? But why would your chauffeur be driving Caroline about?'

'Exactly what I'd like to know.'

Frowning, she asked quietly, 'If you have a chauffeur, why did you need me to drive you to Yorkshire?'

'Because David was on holiday in Spain—or supposed to have been. Only if you saw him at Caroline's house, quiet obviously he wasn't.'

His tone might be mild, his face expressionless, but if it was his chauffeur who had been at Caroline's she wouldn't like to be in his shoes. With a little shiver, she returned her attention to the scenery. And if it was his chauffeur? What then? A confrontation, that was what, a real fun time in fact, and until she could find a way of getting herself back to London it looked as though life was going to be decidedly unpleasant.

'You can take that look off your face, Neile,' he commented, sounding hatefully virtuous. 'It's all your own fault.'

'Why is it? I didn't tell your chauffeur to play both ends against the middle. All I did was drive you up to Yorkshire and get myself embroiled in your domestic disputes. I feel as though I'm going to my execution, and I can't even say that the condemned ate a hearty breakfast, because I didn't. I had two mouthfuls of tea before even that sustenance was denied me.'

'My heart bleeds,' he retorted unfeelingly. 'You surely didn't expect to be welcomed with open arms? If you hadn't played up to Caroline, none of this would have happened.'

Deciding there wasn't any answer to that, she stared stonily through the windscreen. And if there hadn't been the contretemps with Caroline would Mackenzie have got in touch with her, Neile? Glancing at him sideways, she wondered if she had the courage to ask him. And if he said no? Where did that leave her? Giving a long sigh, she then blinked in surprise as he turned into a narrow path between high banks that practically scraped the car either side before it widened out in front of an old stone house that looked as though it had been there forever. The front wall was heavily overgrown with ivy, red and green leaves cascading prettily across grey stonework. Around each window it had been tidily clipped away which gave the odd impression of a myopic old gentleman peering out of a bushy beard and eyebrows.

'Welcome to Castle Frankenstein,' he murmured drily as he watched her changing expressions.

'That's exactly what it feels like,' she agreed despondently. Turning to face him, she entreated, 'Please let me go back to London.'

'No,' he denied softly. 'Stay here for a minute.' Opening his door, he walked off round the side of the house, leaving Neile prey to all sorts of conflicting worries, not least of which was the thought of having to face the chauffeur. If it had been him following her, he'd recognise her as well, which meant he would know damned well why she was there.

Thankful for at least a short reprieve she occupied her time counting the windows, which as a pastime left a lot to be desired but did at least stop her thoughts from gravitating into terrors of the unknown. At least there weren't any bars on the windows; probably the dungeons were round the back, she thought only half humorously.

'And what little horrors are you imagining now?' Mackenzie asked softly from beside her open window.

With a little start, she glared at him. 'Do you have to creep up on people?'

'I didn't creep, and if you hadn't been so preoccupied you'd have heard me easily,' he commented with a slight smile as he opened her door for her. 'So what were you so busily scheming?'

'I wasn't the scheming anything! I was wondering where the dungeons were!'

'In the basement, of course, where else would one have dungeons?' he asked whimsically as he scooped her out and held her easily in his arms. 'It's a tempting thought, Neile,' he added softly as he stared down into her wide blue eyes. 'I could put you in the iron maiden, of course, or on the rack. . .'

'Yes, and I wouldn't put that past you!'

'Wouldn't you?' he asked softly.

Shaking her head, sending the cloud of dark hair to tangle against the collar of his jacket, she swallowed hard, her eyes fixed on his, a trace almost of fear in their depths. She moistened parched lips and her breath jerked to a halt as his eyes followed the movement; she didn't know if it was her overwrought imagination that made him seem closer, or whether he had actually leaned towards her, but whatever it was it was having a very unsettling effect on her nerves. 'Don't,' she whispered huskily.

'Don't what, Neile? Make you fall in love with me? Could I do that, I wonder? Make you my slave—and then discard you. . . How does that scenario appeal?'

'It doesn't,' she managed, her words a mere puff of sound.

'Why? Because it would be too easy? Is that it? Don't they say prisoners often fall in love with their captors?'

'I don't know.' But did captors ever fall in love with their prisoners? No, she decided unhappily, or certainly not in this instance. Too much had happened between them for that ever to occur. Hastily pushing the thought aside, because it was something she so desperately wanted, she tilted her chin defiantly. It wasn't only that he was tall, broad-shouldered, dark and brooding in the classical mould of heroes, nor even that he was exceptionally good-looking in a carved, granite sort of way; it was more something within himself, an aura of power. Even had he been a small man she doubted he would ever have been overlooked or ignored. No, Mackenzie definitely had that certain indefinable something that would make him special no matter what he looked like. But how many women was he special to?

'Like what you see?' he asked humorously.

'No,' she denied automatically as she tried very hard to hold his gaze. 'So am I your prisoner?'

'Perhaps.' His mouth quirking slightly, he added. 'Why not look upon it as being a voluntary patient needing therapy?'

'I don't want to look on it at all,' she derided, 'and certainly not as therapy!'

With a faint smile, he began carrying her towards the house, then halted as they both heard a car moving down the lane behind them.

'Well, Neile,' he said softly, 'it would seem your suspense is nearly at an end. Here comes David now.'

Glancing over his shoulder, she watched the small red car as it passed them and parked beside the front door of the house. With a little flare of panic, she struggled for release.

'Keep still,' he commanded mildly, but with every intention of being obeyed. 'You will do nothing, say nothing. Do you understand? If he asks you any questions, you will say that we met accidentally, that you are merely here because you hurt your foot. Is that clear? Whatever I say, you will go along with—and don't suddenly exclaim. "That's him!"'

'Give me a little credit for some sense,' she said scornfully. Dragging her eyes from his, she looked towards the house and was just in time to see Daniel climb from the rear of the car and stand solemnly, his brown eyes enormous as he watched them. Instead of grinning or running to meet his father as a normal child might have done, he seemed wary and unsure of himself. Was that what she had helped do to him? Killed any spontaneity he might have had? Mackenzie was watching him too, and she felt a lump form in her throat at the expression of defeat in his eyes. His smile was warm and friendly, but his eyes gave his apparent ease the lie.

'Hi, Daniel,' she called brightly, over-brightly, and was rewarded with a cautious smile. Flicking her eyes beyond the boy, to the chauffeur who was standing behind him, she tried to make her look casual. He had fair hair, and he was tall, but beyond that she couldn't be sure. She had never seen the fair-haired man at close quarters and perhaps it would be better to view this man from a distance to get a better perception.

Clutching frantically at Mackenzie's shoulder as he began walking towards his son, she felt a moment of alarm that the wretched man was going to confront the chauffeur there and then, although she should have known better. Mackenzie never did anything he was expected to do.

'David,' he greeted with a slight smile and a nod of dismissal, then waited until the chauffeur had moved away before looking down at Daniel. 'Hi,' he said easily, yet Neile detected the strain in his voice. 'Been somewhere nice?'

'We went to the shops,' he explained quietly, his eyes not quite meeting his father's, then, bringing out one hand from behind his back, he showed them the paper bag he was carrying. 'It's Ned's birthday tomorrow.'

'And you've been to buy her a present?' Neile asked gently.

'Yes.' Staring at her, a look that seemed far too adult for a small boy, he asked seriously, 'Have you hurt your foot?'

'Yes; silly, isn't it? I fell off a step and your father's having to carry me around like a sack of old potatoes.' Pinning a bright smile on her face, she wondered in disgust how she could have said anything so inane, but there was something very off-putting about being stared at so searchingly by this young-old child.

'Does it hurt?' he asked solemnly.

'Mmm, a bit,' she answered as she wondered how much longer they were going to stand out here on the path in the chill wind. 'I——'

'Open the door, will you, Daniel?' Mackenzie interrupted as though he knew exactly what she had been thinking. 'My sack of potatoes is suddenly getting very heavy.' As Daniel hurried to do his bidding, he added softly, so that only she would hear, 'And more than a little agitated if I don't miss my guess. I hope you haven't been lying to me, Neile.'

Giving him a startled glance, she chewed absently on her lower lip while she absorbed the implications of that little statement. What if she decided it *was* David? And he denied it? And Caroline did too? What then? That hadn't occurred to her, and it should have done. 'I didn't lie, Mackenzie,' she insisted quietly as he carried her inside and through a door on his left.

Leaning over the back of the chintz-covered sofa, he lowered her on to the cushions. Remaining bowed over her, he answered equally quietly. 'I do hope not, Neile, for your own sake. So was it him? David?'

'I don't know,' she confessed uncertainly. 'It's like him, and yet. . .But if it is him, and he denies it, what then?' she asked worriedly. 'Will you take his word for it?'

'No. I no longer take people on trust.'

Recognising the rebuke for what it was, she looked away from the bright intentness of his eyes.

'I shall check and double check,' he continued quietly. Straightening, he added, 'I'll get Ned to make you some tea. Can you manage to eat something?'

'Just a couple of biscuits, please.'

When he'd gone, she turned her gaze to the fire. A vastly different fire from the one in the house. Which hadn't had brass fenders or scowling fire-dogs polished to a high shine. The logs in that one hadn't stayed tidily in the grate either; here the coal was probably too well bred to move; and he hadn't needed to rub it in about checking and double checking, had he? That had been just plain nasty. Carefully moving her foot to overhang the edge of the sofa, she eased herself into a sitting position. She then stuffed a cushion behind her back and glanced round the room. It was too tidy, formal, as though it was rarely used, or only on special occasions. Was she a special occasion? she wondered. The thought didn't bring her any comfort.

CHAPTER SEVEN

HEARING the door open, Neile turned her head, and her spirits sank further as she took in the expression on the face of the woman who entered. She was around fifty, dark hair liberally sprinkled with grey, and dour. The housekeeper, no doubt. She'd presumably had chapter and verse about her behaviour from Mackenzie and in consequence had been tried and condemned.

'Thank you,' she said quietly as a tray was placed on her lap with scant regard for her injury. Without answering, or even really acknowledging her presence apart from a look of dislike, the woman went away again leaving Neile to survey the two digestive biscuits that glared back at her from a doily-covered plate. Her words had obviously been taken literally, a couple being two, exactly two and not a crumb more. In other circumstances she might have been amused, only it wasn't other circumstances, and the feeling of being a leper hurt. Her face bleak, she put the two sugar lumps she'd been given into her tea, and stirred it slowly. Whatever happened to innocent until proven guilty?

When she'd drunk the tea and eaten the two biscuits, she put the tray on the floor and leaned back into the corner of the sofa. Staring at the exquisite ormulu clock on the mantelpiece, she watched the little black, well-bred hands tick slowly round. Was this to be her punishment? Left alone? Ignored? As she lay there, the sky outside turned from grey to black; the fire settled and burned low, and gradually her lids drooped and she fell into an uneasy sleep. She was unaware of the housekeeper coming in to remove the tray, or of Daniel creeping in to look at her until softly called out by his father, and she only stirred and lifted weighted lids as strong arms picked her up and carried her upstairs to a softly lit bedroom.

'How do you feel?' he asked neutrally as he lay her on the bed.

'Do you care?' she asked with soft reproach as she stared up at him. 'I could have died down there for all the notice anyone took of me.'

'Oh, dear,' he taunted, 'what a pity you didn't, then you would have been fully justified in your resentment and we would have been mortified by our uncaring behaviour.'

'Oh, shut up.' Turning her face away from the bright mockery of his eyes, she stared miserably at the wall. She couldn't ever remember feeling so helpless and uncared for, yet now that she had company she didn't want it, only to be left alone. 'Go away, Mackenzie, take your sarcasm to someone who might appreciate it.'

'My, my, we are feeling sorry for ourselves, aren't we?' he retorted softly as he went out.

Much to her surprise, five minutes later he was back, with even less sympathy. 'For goodness' sake, Neile, pull yourself together, do. You look like a wet weekend.'

'I feel like a wet weekend,' she muttered. 'How else should I feel? I want to go home.'

'Well, you can't,' he said unfeelingly, 'so stop sulking. Here, I brought you some soup.'

'How thoughtful,' she derided sarcastically as she hauled herself upright. 'The least I expected was bread and water.'

'Which it will be,' he warned, 'if you don't stop making cracks like that.' Putting the tray carefully across her thighs, he regarded her silently for a moment before going across to draw the dusky pink curtains across the window. 'No bars, you see,' he quipped softly before leaning back against the wall, arms folded across his chest.

Ignoring him, she picked up her spoon. She was so

hungry she could have wolfed it down in seconds and had to force herself to eat slowly.

'Feel better now?' he asked in amusement as she leaned back with a little sigh of contentment.

'Yes, thank you.'

'Want some apple pie?' he persuaded softly, then gave a reluctant laugh when her eyes lit up. Taking the tray, he went out, to return seconds later with a dish of apple pie and cream. Perching on the edge of the bed, he watched her eat.

Ignoring his disturbing presence as best she might, she scraped the bowl clean before leaning back against the headboard. Licking the last morsel from her lips, she gave him a cautious smile. 'Thank you.'

'Think we were going to starve you into submission?' he asked humorously.

'Submission?' she queried haughtily.

'A figure of speech only,' he comforted, that wicked mockery still dancing in his eyes.

'I'm very glad to hear it. Is the prisoner allowed to have a bath?'

'Of course.' Turning his head, he nodded towards a door in the wall. 'Through there. Can you manage on your own?'

'Yes,' she said quickly, too quickly, and he gave another grunt of laughter. Staring at him, she wanted to tell him to laugh properly. Not the amused grunts that issued from him from time to time, but a real belly-laugh. When he got up and walked into the bathroom, her eyes followed him. It wasn't very likely. Even if everything was resolved, she doubted she would ever get the chance to know him properly, as she would have liked to, she admitted to herself; as she needed to. She had thought once, when they first met, that he had been as attracted to her as she to him. Felt that curiously familiar excitement, as though they had met before, in another life perhaps, another age. She would have to ask Ellen to give her a forecast, she thought with a faint, sad smile. She'd also better ask her if Ariens and Librans were destined to be star-crossed lovers. Becoming aware of the sound of running water, she swung her legs over the side of the bed.

'Don't get your foot wet,' he instructed as he came to lean in the bathroom doorway and watch her.

'No,' she agreed. Tearing her eyes away from the mesmeric quality of his, she hunted desperately round the room in the hope of finding a robe or something that she could wear.

'What's wrong?'

'Wrong? What should be wrong?' she asked acidly. 'I was looking to see if there was a robe or something that I could borrow.' Swinging her gaze back to him she burst out crossly, 'I don't even have a comb!'

'All taken care of,' he said mildly. 'Ned's looking you out some things now. A nightie, robe, toothbrush. . .'

'Oh,' she mumbled awkwardly, 'that's kind of her.'

'Yes,' he agreed softly, and she looked at him sharply.

'Especially as she doesn't like me, you mean. . .'

'Did I say that?' Making no attempt to move, he continued to watch her until she squirmed in embarrassment.

'Don't,' she mumbled. 'I know I look a wreck.'

'I didn't say that either,' he added in a tone that was almost caressing.

Overwhelmingly aware of the tension that had suddenly invaded the room, she felt heat steal into her cheeks, and looked quickly away. When the silence lengthened, became fearful, she felt her heart lose its rhythm and could think of nothing to say to return things to normal.

'Neile?' he queried softly.

Jerking her gaze back to him, she managed huskily. 'What?'

'What's wrong?'

'Nothing!' she denied. 'Will you go and find those things for me, please?'

An eternity later, he moved, walked across to the door, and as he opened it she heard him say something to someone outside before coming back to her with a robe and nightie across his arm, a comb, toothbrush and tube of toothpaste in his hand. Dropping them on to the bed beside her, he kept his eyes on her flushed face.

Her gaze averted, she quickly gathered them up and held them defensively against her.

'There are towels in the bathroom. . .'

'I'll only need a small one,' she said stupidly, 'I don't want to make more work for your housekeeper than necessary.'

'Mrs Needham won't mind, she——'

'Of course she'll mind!' she interrupted, wondering at his stupidity. Good God, the woman had hated her on sight, surely he must have been aware of that.

'Don't be ridiculous! We do have such sophisticated equipment as washing-machines. Anyone would think Ned had to voyage down to the stream and beat them against the rocks!'

Giving him a look of disgust, she raised her injured foot and began to undo the safety-pin that secured the bandage.

'Now what are you doing?' he asked in exasperation.

'Taking the bandage off—what does it look like? And I wish you'd just go away and leave me in peace!'

'Neile,' he warned as he leaned over and gripped her wrist to stop her, 'leave the bandage alone.'

'No!' she gritted, wrenching herself out of his hold. 'It's too tight!' And suddenly it seemed the most important thing in the world to get the wretched bandage off, because maybe, in doing that, it would release the tension and awareness that was bunching her muscles, twitching at her nerves. Wrenching agitatedly at the pin, hurting her foot in the process, she whimpered as Mackenzie grasped both her hands in his.

'Leave the bandage alone, Neile!' he ordered as he

bent her backwards away from her foot until she was flat against the banked pillows.

Staring up at him as he loomed over her, her eyes too bright, her hair tangled round her flushed face, she froze when his expression changed, became arrested. She hardly noticed the pain in her wrists where he was gripping them so tightly; hardly noticed anything except the feeling of sick excitement in her stomach.

'Want and hate are a contradiction in terms,' he said unexpectedly, his words soft and emotive, and yet his voice was expressionless, denying the feeling of either.

'Wanting isn't always synonymous with liking,' she whispered huskily as she continued to stare at him almost fearfully. His nearness was an oppression that robbed her of sense. She wanted him to move—yet wanted him to stay. 'You aren't the only one full of contradictions, Mackenzie.'

'Meaning you don't like me either, but still want me,' he murmured provocatively.

'No!' she exclaimed, shocked.

'Liar,' he taunted as he slowly released her and straightened.

'It is not a lie!' she insisted forcefully. 'I don't want you!'

With a look of derision, he turned away. 'Take your damned tablets and go and have your bath.'

'I don't want my damned tablets! And I don't want you! My God, but you're arrogant!' she retorted disgustedly.

'Then we make a good pair, don't we? And leave the bandage on!' Striding out, he slammed the door.

'Pig!' And why was he being so picky all of a sudden? Refusing to even think about the few moments of tension on the bed, she defiantly unwound the bandage from her ankle and gave a sigh of relief as the restricting elastic was removed. Suddenly remembering that the taps had been left running, she hopped agitatedly across to the bathroom. God, that would be the next drama, flooding the house. That would go down well. Seeing the water creeping relentlessly past the overflow, she launched herself at the taps and managed to turn them off before any real damage was done.

When she'd collected the things Ned had lent her, the first thing she did was clean her teeth and run the comb through her hair. Undressing and folding her clothes on the bathroom stool, she climbed carefully into the bath and gave an ecstatic sigh as warm water lapped her stiff limbs. Leaning back, she closed her eyes and allowed herself to relax. For the first time in days, she felt almost at peace, and sent up a little prayer of thanks to whoever had invented hot baths. Bliss. Gently wriggling her bad ankle experimentally and finding that the pain was at least bearable, she settled herself for a long soak.

'Neile,' Mackenzie drawled softly, and she snapped her eyes open in shock.

'Get out!' she shrieked. Hastily folding her arms across her naked breasts, she lost her precarious balance in the large bath and, with a yelp of alarm, slid under the water. Spluttering and coughing, she dragged herself upright. 'Don't you dare laugh, you—voyeur!' she screeched. 'How dare you come in without knocking? Get out of here!'

'Calm down,' he soothed mildly, one hand held out placatingly. 'I only came to make sure you hadn't drowned—not from any humane viewpoint, I might add, merely because, should you have done so, odds are that I would have been accused of committing the foul deed, much as I might sometimes want to.'

'It might almost be worth it to see you swing!' she retorted furiously. 'And, now that you've saved me, I'd been enormously grateful if you'd just go away—and stop dangling that piece of bandage as thought it were some form of enticement for me to get out!'

'I told you to leave it on,' he reproved softly as he advanced further into the room.

'Mackenzie. . . Mackenzie!' she yelled, her eyes round

with surprise and alarm as he casually leaned over and pulled out the plug. 'Don't you dare!' she screeched as she grabbed hold of it and tried to put it back. 'You bastard! You rotten, lousy, interfering moronic bastard!'

Easily removing her fingers from the plug, he looped it casually round one of the taps.

Glaring at him, she scrabbled to reach the towel which was just out of reach of her searching fingers, then thumped agitatedly at his thigh when he only continued to regard her with amusement. 'Don't just stand there! Pass me the bloody towel!'

'Language, language,' he tutted reprovingly. Casually reaching for one of the fluffy pink towels from the radiator, he held it just out of reach. 'Come on, Neile, out you get,' he commanded softly.

Temper momentarily overcoming her embarrassment, she levered herself to her feet. As soon as she was balanced she made a grab for the towel, then wobbled precariously when he refused to release it and had no other option except to grab his shoulders to stop herself falling. 'I hate you,' she gritted as he wrapped her in the soft folds.

With a grin that she could only describe as evil, he lifted her out and carried her into the bedroom. Sitting her on the edge of the bed, he returned to the bathroom for the robe and nightie. As she rubbed herself dry she wondered what he was playing at. He'd said himself that he disliked her, didn't trust her, so why the need for games? Certainly he wasn't going about it in a very logical way if he was trying to make her fall in love with him, as he had threatened earlier, and why should he bother anyway? Unable to come up with a satisfactory answer, which also infuriated her, she watched with resentment as he walked back into the bedroom.

'Arms up,' he instructed as he held her nightdress above her open at the hem.

Setting her mouth in a prim line, she did as he said. If

she didn't they'd only enter into another pointless argument. As soon as the cotton decently covered her, he whipped away the towel, then hoisting her to her feet, he pulled back the bedclothes and pushed her backwards so that she fell awkwardly against the pillows.

'Now. Foot.'

'I don't want the bandage back on. I told you——'

'Foot,' he repeated softly, his eyes holding hers. 'Either voluntarily or not, Neile, this bandage goes back on.'

'No, it doesn't. And since when have you been a damned intern?'

'Ah, there are a lot of things you don't know about me, my love, doctoring being one of them.'

'You were never a doctor,' she denied with no idea whether he had or hadn't, 'so don't tell lies—and I am not your love.'

'How true. . .'

'And even if you were in the medical profession, in whatever menial capacity, if you behaved like this you were probably slung out for malpractice or interfering with female patients! And will you please stop urging me under the covers? I'm quite capable of getting into bed by myself!'

With a look of such utter blandness that it made her grit her teeth together, he sat on the edge of the mattress, picked up her foot and rested it across his thighs before saying very, very softly, 'Shut up.'

Snorting inelegantly, she raked the wet hair off her face while he proceeded to re-bandage her foot, and she had to admit, reluctantly, that he did it efficiently. Not that it made any difference, because the minute his back was turned it was coming off again. Grabbing the towel that he'd left on the bed, she began to rub her hair dry, an expression of polite suffering on her beautiful face.

Glancing at her from the corner of his eye, he shook his head. 'No,' he said softly as though he knew perfectly well what she had been thinking. 'The bandage stays on.'

'Did I say differently?' she asked aloofly.

'You didn't need to; your face is an open book, Neile dear.'

'All right, I'll leave it on,' she agreed with pretended capitulation. 'Now go away, Mackenzie.'

'Go away, Mackenzie,' he mimicked. His eyes amused, he fastened the safety-pin in place and tucked her foot under the cover. Getting to his feet, he stood looking down at her. 'Goodnight, Neile,' he said mockingly. 'Sweet dreams.'

'I think they're more likely to be nightmares, don't you?' she asked tartly.

With a little chuckle, he walked towards the door.

'Mackenzie?'

'Mmm?'

'Were you?' she asked curiously.

'Was I what?'

'A doctor!'

Shaking his head, a smile still hovering round his mouth, he denied softly, 'No. But I once did a first-aid course.' Slipping out, he closed the door quietly behind him.

'Rat.' Snapping out the bedside light, she snuggled under the covers, and she had to admit, grudgingly, that he hadn't after all bandaged her foot too tightly, but that was the only thing she would admit. She still disliked him.

The tantalising aroma of frying bacon woke her. Opening her eyes, she blinked to focus them and frowned down at dusky pink carpet two feet from her nose. Somewhat surprised to find herself lying face down across the bed, she considered the matter sleepily for a moment or two before giving up. With a wide yawn she rolled over on to her back and came face to face with Mackenzie.

'Always sleep that way, do you?' he asked in amusement as he helped untangle her from the duvet.

'I'm a restless sleeper—and just what are you doing in my room?' she asked haughtily. 'You shouldn't be here.'

'Why not?' he queried lazily. Making himself at home on the foot of the bed, he grinned when Neile gave another enormous yawn and dragged herself reluctantly upright.

'You look very sexy,' he observed mockingly, 'all warm and flushed with sleep.'

'Really?' she asked with an attempt at indifference. 'How nice.'

'Mmm.' Nodding towards her foot, which was sticking out from under the cover, as was most of her leg, he added, 'I see you kept the bandage on.'

Glancing down, she snatched the cover across her. 'I wish you'd go away—it's too early to play games,' she muttered fretfully.

'It's never too early to play games,' he refuted softly and she looked at him in astonishment.

'You're very full of sweetness and light this morning; just what are you playing at now?' she asked suspiciously.

'Who, me? Nothing. Just being polite.'

'You're never polite. And yesterday I was arch-enemy number one.'

'Ah, that was yesterday. Today I feel more tolerant.'

'Why? You've spoken to the chauffeur?' she demanded, suddenly alert.

'Not yet. I'm working on the rope theory. Actually I came to see if you wanted some breakfast.'

'Yes, please,' she answered automatically. 'What happens if he doesn't hang himself?'

'Then I'll think of something else.'

'If he's guilty,' she added quietly.

'Yes, if he's guilty. Having second thoughts, Neile?'

'I never had any first ones,' she said absently. 'I told you, I couldn't be sure. Mackenzie?' she called as he

walked towards the door. 'What will you do if it isn't
your chauffeur?'

'Go and see Caroline,' he threw over his shoulder as
he went out.

Oh, sure, she thought derisively, you'll get a lot of
sense out of her. She could just imagine that scenario.
Caroline, my love, could you please tell me who the fair-
haired man is that Miss Markham insists has been
following her? Huh. Or maybe not. Maybe he often went
to see Caroline. . . Only that wasn't a thought that
pleased her. Yet it was entirely possible, wasn't it? She'd
once had the suspicion that Mackenzie was still a little in
love with his wife, despite her behaviour. Would a messy
divorce have killed that? She didn't even know if
Caroline had access to Daniel. With a despondent sigh,
she stared gloomily at the door. She was still sitting there
worrying about it when Mackenzie returned carrying a
tray.

'Stop worrying about it,' he instructed shortly as he
put the tray across her knees, 'and eat that while it's
hot.'

He was back to his peremptory tone, she noticed with
a grimace. Picking up her knife and fork, she began on
her eggs and bacon. 'I could have come downstairs for
it; there's no need to wait on me, you know.'

Ignoring her, he perched back on the foot of the bed
and watched her thoughtfully. 'Why have you never
married?' he asked abruptly. 'Most women your age are,
or at least engaged. It can't be for lack of offers.'

Staring at him in astonishment, she snapped crossly,
'Mind your own business—it has nothing whatsoever to
do with you and I have absolutely no desire to discuss
my love-life, or lack of it.' Not that her reluctance would
make much difference to Mackenzie, she thought sourly,
he didn't seem to have heard of minding his own
concerns. 'And what do you mean, my age? I'm only
twenty-seven, for goodness' sake, hardly in my dotage!'

'And the offers?' he persisted.

'What offers?' she scoffed. 'Anyone would think men were queuing up for my hand!'

'And weren't they?'

'Of course not! Why the hell should they?'

'Why indeed?' he murmured silkily. 'Especially if you talk to them the way you talk to me.'

Giving him a look of irritation, she put her knife and fork tidily on her plate, and picked up her tea. Cradling the cup between her palms, she sipped slowly.

'So?' he persevered.

'Oh, for goodness' sake! I thought you'd have had more sense, but you seem to be making the same assumptions as everyone else!'

'Ah,' he exclaimed softly with a little nod. 'They don't line up because they assume someone who looks like you must already be spoken for. Yes?'

'Yes. Or that I'm promiscuous. It's really rather a catch-22 situation.'

'Mmm, so you went the other way,' he agreed in sudden understanding, then grinned when she looked appalled. 'Not that other way! So that's why you were so fidgety in Yorkshire. You did expect me to leap on you, despite my denials. . .'

'No,' she countered primly, then felt herself go pink, because that was exactly what she had thought, at first anyway. He made her sound incredibly vain, and she wasn't, not really. 'It isn't easy, you know,' she sighed. 'I sometimes wish I were plain. Girlfriends I used to go out with got fed up with all the boys gravitating towards me—it isn't funny!' she snapped when he grunted with laughter.

'No, sorry,' he said, not looking sorry at all. 'And I suppose the same applied to married friends? Wives thinking you were about to rush off with their husbands?'

'Something like that,' she admitted. 'So I don't go out very much. Not like it bothers me,' she added quickly.

'I have the agency to run and that takes up most of my time and energy.'

Sounding as though he was trying very hard not to laugh, he asked, 'And you've never. . .?'

'I didn't say I'd never! Just that I wasn't promiscuous. Anyway, why on earth can it matter to you why I've never married or got engaged?'

'It doesn't,' he agreed mildly, 'I was just curious. So did you?'

'Did I what?' she asked, exasperated.

'Want to get married?'

'No,' she lied. If he thought she was going to bare her soul to him, he was in for another think. She had no intention of telling him about her past. 'And you don't need to look at me like that. Not everyone wants to get married, settle down into domesticity and have children.'

'No, but you don't seem the type to enjoy having a string of lovers with no commitment. . .'

'I do not have a string of lovers!'

'. . .nor are you the type to enjoy remaining celibate.'

'Will you kindly go away and stop baiting me, Mackenzie?' she demanded wrathfully as she slammed her cup back in the saucer. 'It's none of your damned business!'

'The lady doth protest too much, methinks,' he quoted softly. 'What happened? Someone run out on you?'

'Oh, good grief! Why do men persist in these weird and wonderful psychologies? Just because a woman isn't married you automatically assume she must have been jilted or had an unhappy experience. And instead of worrying about my hang-ups you'd do better to go and sort out your own!'

'Like?' he asked softly.

'Like lack of trust for one!'

'But I don't suffer from lack of trust,' he denied, his voice very quiet, 'and as soon as you prove trustworthy I'll trust you, but until then. . .'

'Until then,' she gritted, 'you'll go on baiting me!'

'Is that what I'm doing, Neile?'

'Well, isn't it?'

'No. I told you, I was just curious about you. . .'

'Or piqued. . .' she said thoughtfully as she remembered something his ex-wife had once said. 'Is that it, Mackenzie? Because I made it quite clear that I didn't fancy you?'

Looking genuinely puzzled, he shook his head. 'Is that what you think? My little ego was bruised?'

'Well, isn't it?'

'No.' With an infectious chuckle that thoroughly surprised her, he asked slowly, 'Is that the impression I give?'

'No,' she had to admit, 'it was something Caroline said, the reason she gave for not believing we hadn't slept together at the cottage. She asked if I seriously expected her to believe that Super Stud hadn't made a pass at me.'

'Super Stud?' he echoed on a choke of laughter. 'Oh, my.' Moving too swiftly for her to evade, he lounged forwards, one arm either side of her, effectively trapping her. 'Well, now, Neile,' he growled softly, 'a taunt like that cannot be allowed to go unchallenged, now can it?'

'I didn't say it!' she yelped. 'She did! How the hell would I know what sort of—er. . .?'

'Stud?' he asked helpfully. 'But it seems to have made you wonder. . .'

'It has not!' she denied forcefully.

'Then why say it? Because saying it, Neile, my love, makes it sound as though you have doubts about my prowess.'

'I don't have doubts because I haven't thought about it!' she ground out. 'But apparently your darling ex-wife did, because I seem to remember you saying that Caroline was unfaithful. Hardly the actions of a satisfied woman, would you say?' she taunted. Expecting him to be furious, she was totally astonished when he laughed. He sounded so genuinely amused that she could only

stare at him, nonplussed. 'Well, would you?' she asked
weakly.

'Yes,' he agreed, 'but not I think because I couldn't
satisfy her. I hesitate to say it, Neile, but she only took
lovers after I had lost interest in her as a womnan, in an
effort, I suspect, to make me jealous.'

'Which obviously didn't work,' she derided, trying to
keep her breathing even and failing. 'And I wish you'd
get off me—you're hurting my legs.'

'I'm not touching your legs. Am I touching your
senses, Neile?' he whispered mockingly.

'No! And your feelings, or lack of them, are of
absolutely no interest to me!'

'Is that why you sound as though you've been running?' he asked, a fascinating little smile in his eyes.
'Because they're of absolutely no interest to you?'

'If I sound a little agitated,' she said through her teeth,
'it's because I don't like you being so close to me!'

'Why?'

'Because I don't like you!'

'Don't you?' he breathed softly as his head lowered
relentlessly towards hers.

'No,' she denied frantically. 'Mackenzie, please don't
do this to me,' she pleaded desperately. 'It isn't fair.'

'Who wants to be fair? You're one hell of a sexy lady,
you know, and I wouldn't be human if I wasn't tempted.'

'You weren't in Yorkshire,' she pointed out
breathlessly.

'Wasn't I?'

'Were you?' she asked jerkily, with no knowledge that
she was about to ask him that at all.

'Were you?' he countered, then gave a slow smile of
disbelief when she shook her head. 'Liar. Why else were
you so fidgety?'

'I told you, because I expected you to come on all
heavy. . .'

'Tut-tut,' he reproved lightly. 'You were afraid I
would touch you and equally afraid you would respond,

thereby shooting all your arguments down in flames. That was it, wasn't it, Neile?'

Staring at him, refusing to confirm or deny it, even to herself, she drew in her breath sharply when one hand moved slowly to her neck under the fall of hair. 'No,' she whispered.

'Yes. Part your lips, Neile.' When she did so, more from suprirse than anything else, he touched his mouth infinitely gently against hers and an almost unbearable excitement unfurled inside. God, it had been such a long time since anyone had touched her like this, kissed her with such gentleness, and she wouldn't have been human if she hadn't felt the need to respond, to stop fighting.

'I want to undress, Neile,' he breathed against her mouth, 'climb into your warm bed and make love to you, slowly, very, very slowly, with exquisite tenderness, feel your drugged response. . .' Tracing one finger across her mouth, his eyes following the slow, deliberate movement, he continued softly, 'I like you, Neile Markham.' With a faint smile, he raised his eyes to hers. 'Shouldn't admit that, should I? But it's true. I don't want to be wrong about you. . .'

'You are. . .'

'. . .I want to believe in your innocence because I want to get to know you properly. Find the real Neile.' Leaning forwards, he pressed another soft kiss on her parted mouth. 'I enjoy fighting with you, bandying words; there's an excitement about it. . . You make me smile when I don't want to; you make me ache—and I don't want to do that either. After our trip to Yorkshire, I found myself thinking about you. Your face would rise before me at meetings; in the car; in bed—and I want you very, very much.' With a deep, slow breath, he gathered her against him, tilted her head against his shoulder, looked down into her wide bemused eyes, and smiled. 'Say it,' he ordered softly.

'Say what?' she asked weakly, her body fluid and melting.

'That you want me too.'

Searching his face, his unusual eyes, she allowed her gaze to travel to his mouth. Close enough to just reach out and touch, she thought hazily. Just a fraction away, and her own mouth parted in unconscious need; her heart beat just that little bit faster. Raising her eyes to his, she breathed unevenly. 'I want you.'

The words were barely out before he bridged the tiny gap, moved his mouth seductively on hers, smoothed his palm down her back, round to her waist and halted against her ribcage. Her breath locking in her throat, she moaned, and his palm completed the short journey to the heavy fullness of her breast.

Pressing against him, her arms holding him close, she breathed in the scent of him, the warmth, the need. His kisses were drugging, mesmerising, expert, and she wanted him, knew she always had, from the first moment they'd looked at each other in her mother's garden.

Sliding her arms up his warm back, she touched her fingers to his nape, and he shuddered against her and lifted his head. Keeping her eyes closed, she only opened them when he blew softly on the lids.

'Not now, Neile,' he said softly as he gazed down into her warmly flushed face. 'Not now,' he repeated, sounding regretful.

'Not?' she asked achingly.

'No.' With a firm gesture, he put her away from him and stood up.

Staring at him, her eyes blank, uncomprehending, she gave a little shudder. 'Why?' she whispered. 'Because I haven't proved myself trustworthy?'

'Perhaps. Can you blame me?'

'And if you find I haven't lied? You'll fulfil your promise? Is that it?'

When he didn't answer, only continued to watch her, she looked away. Grabbing the cover, she pulled it across her. 'Get out of here,' she said quietly.

With a sound that might have been regret, he picked

up the tray and walked out, pulling the door to behind him with his foot.

How clinical. 'Bastard,' she whispered. Throwing herself back against the pillows, she stared at the closed door. Refusing to acknowledge that he had every reason to be mistrustful of women, all she could think about was that he'd deliberately aroused her and left her aching. Well, if he could be so damned calculating, switch his emotions on and off like a tap, he could leave them off! He wouldn't get the chance to play his games again. Oh, no. Not any more, Mackenzie, she promised herself. You take me as I am or go without!

Hearing a movement out on the landing, she looked up, her face determined. If he'd come back with second thoughts. . .then let her breath out in a disappointed sigh as the door was pushed hesitantly open to reveal Daniel, a large book clutched to his chest.

Forcing a smile, she greeted softly, 'Hello, come to keep me company?'

With a funny little nod, he came further into the room and walked to stand beside the bed, his dark brown eyes fixed unwaveringly on hers.

'Come on,' she said gently, patting the bed in encouragement, 'I don't bite, you know.' Not children anyway, but she'd damned well like to bite his father.

Moving to where she indicated, he climbed up to sit stiffly beside her.

Taking his book, she laid it flat on her knees. 'This is a nice book,' she enthused brightly. 'Can you read?'

'A bit,' he volunteered with a shy smile. 'I go to school now.'

'Do you?' she asked warmly, trying to sound impressed. She assumed he must mean nursery; he was hardly old enough to go to proper school. 'Do you like it?'

Staring at her as though he really needed to give the question a lot of thought before he answered, he finally gave a little nod. 'Yes.'

Grinning and hugging the warm body to her, she dropped a spontaneous kiss on his dark hair. 'Good. Going to read me a story?'

'No,' he said solemnly. 'It has a deer.' Leaning across her, he opened the book at the relevant page.

Rather touched, she looked down, then smiled. It was exactly like the one they'd seen in Sussex. 'Have you seen any more?' she asked gently.

'No,' he said slowly. Looking up into her eyes, he asked carefully. 'Will you be here in the spring?'

'You remembered what I said?' she asked in surprise, and for some odd, silly reason felt a lump form in her throat so that she had to cough to clear it. 'No, darling, I shan't be here in the spring.' Seeing his disappointment, she offered impulsively, 'But, if Daddy will let me, I'll come up then and we'll go and see if we can find one. How about that?' And was surprised to find how much she meant it.

Searching her face as though seeking the truth of her offer there, he smiled, a heartbreaking little smile that choked her all over again. 'Will Daddy let me?' he asked cautiously.

'Of course he will,' she encouraged. 'Why on earth wouldn't he let you go and see the deer?' He might not be so keen on my participation, she thought sourly, but he sure as hell wouldn't stop his son doing anything he wanted. With a gentle finger beneath his chin, she turned his face up to hers. 'Hmm?'

'Mummy said he wouldn't.'

'Mummy said Daddy wouldn't let you see the deer?' she asked, puzzled.

'Yes, but I'm not 'sposed to tell you,' he whispered, and to her horror she saw a tear slide slowly down his cheek.

'Oh, darling, don't cry.' Hugging his small body tight, she bent her face to his. 'Why can't you tell me?'

'Mummy said not to.'

'Not to tell me?' she persisted. She didn't know why

it was important he tell her, just knew that it was. What the hell had Caroline been up to now? 'Did Mummy say you weren't to tell me?'

Staring down at his lap, a frown on his face, he suddenly shook his head. 'No. Not tell Daddy.'

'Well, you won't be telling Daddy, will you? You'll be telling me.' Although telling her what she hadn't the faintest idea, and she wondered if she'd missed some point along the way in their very odd conversation. 'What exactly was it that Mummy said you weren't to tell? That you couldn't see the deer?'

'She said Daddy wouldn't let me.'

'Ah,' she murmured as enlightenment began to dawn. 'Did you tell Mummy about me and the deer?'

'Yes.'

'And that you wanted to see them again?'

'Yes.'

Cow, she thought, then wondered how to explain to Daniel that it wasn't anything to do with him or the deer, but his darling mother trying to prevent Mackenzie coming into contact with herself. Stupid woman. Before she could even attempt to get a suitable reply into order, he added softly. 'Because he bought me.'

'What?'

'Because he bought me,' he explained again solemnly as though that explained everything very clearly.

'Who bought you?'

'Daddy.'

Thoroughly confused, she stared at him for a moment before trying again. 'Daniel,' she began gently, 'I don't think I quite understand. Mummy said Daddy bought you?'

'Yes. From her. She said I wouldn't be able to see the deers, or have a bike or a puppy, because he bought me.'

'She said this to you?' she asked, appalled.

'Yes. I asked if I could have a puppy and she said no, and then I knocked over my milk and she was cross, and she said Daddy wouldn't let me have anything, because he didn't love me, he'd only bought me.' Looking up at her, his face unnaturally serious for one so young, Neile didn't think she had ever felt so angry or helpless in her entire life.

Keeping her expression neutral with an effort, she asked gently, 'Does Daddy know? That she said all that to you?'

With a funny little shrug that was such an adult gesture, he looked down again.

Dear God, Mackenzie, and you blamed me? Shifting herself slightly so that she could see Daniel's face, she placed her hands on his shoulders and looked into his eyes. 'I'm not trying to tell you that Mummy didn't say what you heard, but sometimes, when people are cross, they say things they don't really mean.' Biting her lip as she tried to think of a way of explaining that he would understand, she continued with quiet conviction, 'Your Daddy loves you very much. . .'

'He didn't buy me?'

'Of course he didn't. . .' Only he had, and if she denied it now, and Daniel found out at some later date that she'd lied, with whatever good intentions, his trust would be shattered all over again. 'Well, he did buy you, in a sort of way—I don't know how much of this you will understand, but sometimes grown-ups find they don't like each other very much, like your Mummy and Daddy, so when Daddy left home he wanted to take you with him only Mummy said he couldn't unless he paid her lots of money. So because he wanted you very much, because you were his son and he loved you, he paid Mummy. Do you understand?'

'Yes,' he agreed quietly.

She wasn't altogether sure he did, but she didn't know how else to explain it. It would be better for Mackenzie to do so because, although Caroline was the villain of the piece, Mackenzie might not want his son to know that. 'Well, it doesn't matter now,' she said comfortingly, giving him the warmest smile she could muster. 'All you

need to know is that Daddy loves you very, very much.'
As she spoke, her voice low, soft, she pressed a kiss to
his cheek so that her words were slightly muffled.

'Daniel, your lunch is ready,' Mackenzie said coldly
from the doorway, and they both looked up, Daniel with
a worried look as though fearful of being told off for
doing something wrong, and Neile with dislike and a
renewed simmering of temper as she noticed Daniel's
expression.

'Run along, darling, go and have your lunch; I want a
word with Daddy.'

'About the deers?' he whispered hopefully.

'Yes, about the deer.'

As Daniel scrambled down and went out. Mackenzie
came in and closed the door behind him.

'I want a word with you,' she began ominously as she
closed the book and laid it beside her. 'My God, you talk
about my being criminal. . . What the hell do you think
you're doing?' she exclaimed as he turned the key firmly
in the lock.

'Making sure we won't be interrupted.'

'Well, there's no need to lock the door!'

'There's every need,' he said grimly as he strode over
to the bed and pushed her back down as she struggled
upright. 'And when I want Daniel to know about my
marital squabbles, I'll tell him myself.'

'You heard? Then why the hell didn't you come in
and say so?'

'Because I wanted to know how far you'd go! You
bitch, you bloody little bitch!' he burst out as his fingers
bit cruelly into her arms. 'Why? Just because I kissed
you? Teased you? Is that what this is all about? Get at
me through my son?'

'No!' she exclaimed, appalled that he could even think
such a thing.' 'I——'

'Shut up!'

'Mackenzie! If you'll——'

'I said shut up!' he snarled.

'But it wasn't what you thought——'

'No, I don't suppose it was!' he sneered. 'It would be something much more devious than anything I could imagine.'

'Mackenzie, will you stop jumping to bloody conclusions? And take your hands off me! You're hurting!'

'Hurting? I'd like to kill you!' When she wrenched herself from him, he wrenched her forcibly back. 'Don't you dare turn your back on me!' he spat savagely. 'I believed you! I really believed you were sincere!'

'I was!' she shouted back. Taking a deep breath, she tried again. Putting out a conciliatory hand, she had it knocked violently aside. She gritted her teeth in temper, and insisted, 'Will you damned well listen? If I did wrong——'

'Wrong?' he exploded. 'Wrong? Lord, but you're unbelievable!'

'Me, unbelievable?' she demanded in shock as she scrambled upright. 'Me? You're the one who thinks he has a monopoly on being right! If you'd keep quiet for just two seconds, I could explain——'

'I don't need you to explain! I heard!'

'Oh, God give me strength,' she muttered. Shoving his hand away, she attempted to get to her feet only to be shoved ruthlessly back down again. 'You touch me just once more, Mackenzie,' she warned.

'And what?' he sneered.

'And I'll kick you right where it hurts most,' she threatened. 'I don't think I have ever met a more unreasonable, nasty-minded——'

'Nasty-minded?' he asked, his face thrust close to hers. 'Nasty-minded?' His mouth twisting with contempt, he caught her hair in a painful grip to hold her still, and demanded. 'Did you or did you not just tell my son that I bought him? Well?' he barked.

'Did,' she gritted. 'Now let go of me!' Glaring at him, her eyes dark and angry, her mouth tight, she deliberately lashed out with her foot when he didn't immediately release her. 'I warned you,' she told him when he hissed with pain and released her. When he straightened, she took one look at the implicit threat in his eyes, the reaching hand, and hastily rolled clear, but not quite quickly enough.

CHAPTER EIGHT

'You lay one finger on me. . .' Neile began nervously as Mackenzie hauled her unceremoniously back across the bed.

'Shut up,' he said with soft menace.

'I will not shut up—and if you think you can frighten me by this macho display of strength, let me tell you it doesn't do any such thing! Get off! You'll regret this,' she added warningly as he deliberately placed one knee across her thighs and grabbed both flailing arms at the wrists.

'Not half so much as you will,' he grated softly, 'and so help me, Neile, I've never hit a woman in my life, but you're coming dangerously close. . .'

'So hit me, why don't you?' she taunted as she lay beneath him like a rag doll. 'Be about par for the course, wouldn't it? You've done practically everything else to me!'

'Have I? I haven't even come close to what I could do, so if I were you I'd keep that pretty little mouth closed.'

'But you're not me, are you?' she derided defiantly. 'So what are you going to do now? Rape me?' When he didn't answer, she gave him a look of scorn. She could feel the tension in him, the violence, but was determined not to meekly back down when none of it had been her fault. 'You even so much as breathe on me, Mackenzie, and I'll drag your name through every court in the land. You think you had trouble with Caroline? Well, let me tell you it will be nothing compared to what I'll do!'

'Really?'

'Yes, really.'

His eyes steady on hers, he gave a very nasty smile. 'But I don't intend to lay a finger on you, Neile—and you'd find it very hard to prove rape when you were a willing participant.'

'Willing?' she scoffed incredulously. 'Are you out of your tiny brain?'

'Not at all, Neile. You think I couldn't make you respond?'

Staring at him, her eyes wide, she knew that he could—and the terrible thing was she wanted him to. The tension, the explosive quality about him, excited her. He was no longer even the Mackenzie she knew. This was a cold, controlled stranger, grim and determined, and to her horror she heard herself whisper. 'So make me—and when you find out it wasn't my fault, that it was yours—no,' she whimpered as his grip tightened cruelly.

'Don't you dare,' he said savagely, 'don't you dare tell me again that it's not your fault. I heard you! I stood outside that door and I heard you tell him that I'd bought him. . .'

'But you did!' she exclaimed. 'And he said——'

'I don't want to hear what he said!' he yelled. 'I don't want to hear anything from you ever again! You walked into my life and you systematically and deliberately set out to wreck it!'

'No!'

'Yes!' he hissed. 'And, so help me, I want to destroy you! He's four years old!' he shouted. 'Four! What in God's name are you trying to do to him?'

'I was trying to help him! I was! Oh, for God's sake, Mackenzie, he asked about the deer, asked if I would be here in the spring. What the hell was I supposed to say to that? Then he said you wouldn't let him because Caroline had said so. Because of me. She was jealous, Mackenzie. Vindictive! And don't you dare look at me like that! Whatever else I may do, I don't tell lies!'

Shoving him away, she scrambled quickly to the other side of the bed. Grabbing the bed-head, she hauled herself upright to face him across the mattress. Her breath coming in angry jerks, she retorted furiously, 'You're a fool, Mackenzie, and everything you get you damned well deserve! You wanted me to be guilty. Wanted to punish me for your own shortcomings. Well, good! Go ahead and blame me. I don't care any more. I liked you!' she shouted. 'And, boy, was I wrong!'

'Liked me? Liked me?' he grated as he began to advance round the bed towards her. 'You liked me?' he demanded in disbelief. 'How the hell do you behave to someone you hate? I didn't think there could be anyone else as twisted as Caroline,' he stated grimly as he continued to move towards her, 'but I was wrong, and what in God's name did I ever do to deserve two of you?' Finally reaching her, he put one hand round her neck and pushed her hard up against the wall. 'At least Caroline in her own way was honest; she didn't pretend to be anything but a bitch. But you, you with your winsome smiles, your justifications. . .'

Shoving his hand away, she blazed, 'Not justifications! Explanations! And if you're too dumb, too full of your own importance, to listen, then you can go to hell, Mackenzie Grant!' Putting both hands against his chest, she pushed as hard as she could just as he grabbed her shoulder. Off balance, he dragged her down with him and they both fell against the side of the bed.

'Get off me!' she spat as she tried to untangle herself. Mortifyingly aware of her naked thighs across his legs, she grabbed the quilt and tried to pull herself up, and all she succeeded in doing was to pull the quilt off the bed on top of them. Struggling furiously, hitting out at him wherever he touched her, she tried to get to her feet— and it wasn't his fault, not really, she knew it wasn't, he was in just as much of a temper as she was, but as he tried to push her away, deflect her flailing arm, his fist caught her on the jaw and she fell over backwards. Stunned for a moment by the force of the blow, she blinked up at him as he struggled to his feet.

His breathing laboured, his face twisted into a savage

mask, he breathed, 'Oh, God.' Dropping to his knees beside her, he helped her into a sitting position.

Leaning against him while she got her breath back, she felt all the fight go out of her and she slumped tiredly. Putting out one hand she rubbed it gently across his chest. 'Oh, Mackenzie, this is so stup——'

'Don't!' he said forcefully. Wrenching her hand away, he got to his feet. 'Don't touch me, talk to me—don't even look at me! You make me sick, do you know that? You lied, cheated, used the cheapest weapon of all: your looks. I could have forgiven the other, but not your words to Daniel. Those I can't forgive. Not ever. Now get out of my house.' Striding to the door, he unlocked it and slammed out.

Propped limply against the side of the bed, she stared at the closed door. Emotionally and physically drained, she just sat there. Her bad ankle throbbed unmercifully, and her jaw hurt, but they were as nothing compared to the pain inside. Putting up a shaking hand, she touched her fingers to the side of her face. Oh, Mackenzie. With a long defeated sigh, she got awkwardly to her feet, then whirled round in alarm as the door opened.

'Oh, it's you,' she exclaimed weakly as she saw the housekeeper. Avoiding her eyes, she hopped towards the bathroom. 'I shall be leaving in a few minutes,' she explained shakily. 'Is there a local taxi service, do you know?'

'I believe so; I can look up the number if you wish.'

'Yes, thank you, I'd be very grateful.'

'Are you all right?' the woman asked grudgingly, and Neile wondered what she could see on her own face. Guilt? Shame? Misery? Or did she already have a bruise on her jaw?

'Yes, I'm fine. I'll be down in a few minutes.'

Nodding, the housekeeper turned away, then just as suddenly turned back. 'David could take you——'

'No!' she denied sharply. 'No,' see repeated more moderately. 'I'd rather have a taxi.'

'As you wish.' When the housekeeper had gone, Neile hopped into the bathroom and quickly dressed. Stretching her stocking as wide as she could, she forced it over her bandaged foot. She stood before the mirror and combed her hair, and then just stared at her reflection in shock. She was as white as a sheet, her eyes dark and empty. The only sign of her fight with Mackenzie was a faint red mark on the side of her chin. And you deserved more, Neile. Yes, you did, because you did goad him, and, even while you were fighting with him, part of you wanted him to make love to you. Dear God, what sort of a woman does that make you? All these years being disgusted at the behaviour of men, of being treated as a sex object, accusing them of only wanting you to warm their bed, and what do you do? Do exactly the same to Mackenzie. What happened to your promise to give men a wide berth? Are you some sort of masochist? Is that it? Wasn't Gordon enough for you?

She could have made Mackenzie listen—if she'd really wanted to. Unable to look at herself any longer, see the truth in her dark eyes, she turned hastily away. Picking up her boot, she limped out and downstairs.

The housekeeper was on the phone arranging for the cab, and it wasn't until she replaced the receiver that Neile remembered she didn't have any money, which meant she'd have to borrow some. From Ned. Taking a deep breath in an effort to hide her embarrassment, she asked quietly, 'Do you think you could lend me some money to get back to London?'

Staring rather assessingly at Neile, she finally nodded. 'Will twenty pounds be enough?'

'Yes, thank you. I'll send it back as soon as I get home.'

'There's no hurry; you'd better come and sit down while you wait.'

'Yes. Do you also have a pad or a piece of paper I could have? I need to leave a note for Mackenzie.'

'Why can't you just tell him? He'll be back in a minute, he's only taken Daniel out for a walk.'

'Because we aren't talking,' she said quickly. Looking down, she picked a non-existent piece of fluff from her skirt. And if that wasn't an understatement, she didn't know what was. Damn him. Damn all men for the emotional turmoil they brought in their wake; but she couldn't allow Daniel to be the loser in all this. She'd have to write down all that Daniel had said, and then it was up to Mackenzie.

'I see,' Mrs Needham murmured. 'Well, I'll get you a pad and go and find that money.'

Settling Neile on the sofa, she found a writing-pad and pen in the bureau. Handing them to her, she went out, presumably to get her purse. Opening out the pad, Neile quickly wrote down all that Daniel had said in short, tense sentences, then quickly tore out the page and folded it. Scribbling Mackenzie's name on the front, she handed it to the housekeeper when she came back with the money and to tell her the taxi was here.

'I'll see that he gets it,' the woman said quietly. 'Are you sure you're all right?'

'Yes, I'm sure. Thank you for—putting up with me. Goodbye.'

'Goodbye, miss.'

It didn't take more than twenty minutes to get to the station, and the taxi-driver kindly helped her inside and gave her into the care of a porter who helped her on to the platform.

'Be another ten minutes,' he informed her kindly. 'Want to sit in the waiting-room?'

'No, I'll just lean against a post or something; thanks anyway.'

'OK, miss.'

Bustling off, he left Neile to her bleak thoughts until a loud crash behind her made her look round.

'Of all the damned, bloody stupid places to leave a trolley!' Mackenzie swore as he furiously righted the piece of equipment that he'd just knocked over in his mad dash on to the platform. 'And I don't know what you're smirking at!' he retorted as he rubbed his sore knee and limped across to her.

'Smirking?' she asked hollowly. 'I don't have the energy to smirk, and if you'd been looking where you were going you wouldn't have fallen over it in the first place.'

'If you hadn't rushed off I wouldn't have needed to look where I was going!' Glaring at her, he suddenly looked away, his face flushing. 'Oh, God, Neile, I'm sorry.'

'Don't,' she muttered, and to her everlasting relief she heard the rumble of a train in the distance. Straightening in readiness, clutching her boot like a talisman, she stared agitatedly along the track.

'Neile. . .'

'Go away.'

'Oh, Neile, don't,' he exclaimed helplessly. With a long sigh, he came to stand in front of her. 'I am sorry. Desperately sorry. Sorry!' he exploded with a grimace of distaste. 'What a damned inadequate word that is. It doesn't even cover the half of it, does it? The accusations, the arrogance, the—assault, though why in God's name you couldn't have just told me before. . .' Taking a deep breath, he added more quietly, 'Come back with me. . .'

'No.' Hearing the increased rumble of the train, the faint vibration, she tried to hop round him so that she would be nearer the edge of the platform. She couldn't bear to look at him, see his shame, because it only magnified her own.

'And what about Daniel? What am I supposed to tell him?'

'Oh, that's really fair, isn't it?' she asked bitterly, her agitation forgotten for the moment. 'That's really laying it on the line.'

'I know, but I won't do it to him again, Neile. I can't. He came rushing back from our walk to tell you about the things he'd seen, about a rabbit——'

'Sod the rabbit!'

'Oh, Neile,' he exclaimed on a muffled grunt of laughter. 'I——'

'Don't you "oh, Neile" me! Don't you dare "oh, Neile" me!'

'But he likes you,' he explained with that devastating smile in his eyes. 'I like you. Please come on——'

'No.'

'But I promised Daniel I'd bring you back. Don't make it a lie, Neile. Please don't. He believed me.'

'Oh, that's not fair,' she whispered. 'That's so bloody unfair.'

'I know. I'm fighting with any weapon to hand. For his sake. For my sake.'

'You hurt me,' she breathed, looking down, away from him, anywhere but at him.

'Dear God, do you think I don't know that?' Putting out his hand, he touched a finger incredibly gently to her sore chin. 'Do you think I don't know what I did? What I wanted to do? And do you know what's even worse, Neile? Even thinking those things about you, convinced of your treachery, I wanted you. I wanted to take you, there and then on the floor,' he concluded, a horrified shudder in his voice.

And she would have let him, she thought bleakly, would have helped him to do it. Didn't he know that, for God's sake?

'Neile?' he began again persuasively. 'Come back with me——What?' he swung round to snap irritably as the porter grasped his sleeve.

'Is that your red car out there?' he demanded in outraged accents.

'Yes!'

'Then shift it! *Now*, laddie,' he warned. 'The parcel van can't get in——'

'Then let it wait. I won't be five minutes!'

'Quite right you won't! You'll be five seconds! Those parcels have to be on this train! Now shift!'

'Oh, sod it! Here, you move it,' he muttered, thrusting his car keys at the porter.

'I will not! My insurance don't cover other people's cars.'

'Oh, good grief. Don't you dare go anywhere,' he threatened Neile over his shoulder as he hurried out.

'Damned silly place to leave it,' the porter grumbled as he slowly followed him. 'Half across the yard, door wide open. . .'

Staring down at the boot still clasped to her chest, she gave a shaky sigh. Laddie, she thought with sad humour. Anyone less like a laddie would be hard to imagine. But she wouldn't go back with him. She couldn't. Hearing the train approaching, she straightened again with determination. Her hand out ready, as soon as it halted she grasped the nearest door-handle and pulled it open, then squealed in alarm as she was grabbed from behind.

'You are not getting on this train!' Mackenzie said firmly.

'I am!'

'Neile,' he warned quietly. 'one way or another, you are coming home with me!'

'I am not!' she gasped furiously as she tried to free herself from his grip.

'Yes, you are.' Prising her fingers free of the death-grip she had on the train door, he held on grimly when she tried to pull free. 'And, if I have to, I will sling you over my shoulder and abduct you. This whole farce has gone on long enough. Now, are you coming quietly? Or not?'

'Not,' she said flatly.

'Right.' Shifting his grip, deliberately placing a hand on each of her hips, he stared at her, determination in every line of his face.

'You just dare,' she warned quietly. 'I'll scream. . .'

'So scream.'

Opening her mouth, she choked as a large palm was

placed across it. 'Either voluntarily or not, believe me, you are coming home!'

Holding his gaze, her own defiant, she wrenched his hand away. 'I'm not going,' she said as reasonably as possible in the circumstances. Putting out her arm, she grabbed the train door again.

'Neile,' he said softly, the very faintest twitch to his mouth. 'We can make it easy, or we can make it hard, but have no doubt, we are making it.'

'No, we aren't, and if you're not careful I'll sue you for harassment.'

'You can sue me for whatever you like—later. Right now we don't have time.'

'We have all the time in the world. I'm going to ring Thelma——'

'Thelma doesn't need ringing.'

'Then I'll ring the police.'

Leaning forwards until his nose was practically touching hers, he said softly, 'Move.'

'Are you getting on this train or not?' the exasperated voice of the porter intruded.

'Not,' Mackenzie straightened up to say. With a nasty little smile, he deliberately slammed the door shut. The porter blew the whistle and the train began to draw away.

Staring at him with loathing, her voice pitched as low as his, she said softly, 'I hate you.'

'Good. Can we go now?'

With a haughty sniff, and declining the use of his arm, she hopped towards the exit. Maybe when she was outside in the street she could scream, cause a commotion; surely someone would come to her aid. Swinging through the barrier, her head held high, she manoeuvred herself back down the steps to the forecourt. Apart from a taxi cab, there was no one about, it might have been a Sunday morning for all the movement to be seen. The taxi-driver was leaning against his cab and gave her a faint enquiring smile as she halted before him.

'Good afternoon,' she said with suspect politeness. Forcing herself to smile, she stated clearly, 'I am being abducted against my will.'

'Are you, miss?' he asked cheerfully. 'That's the ticket. All right, sir?' he asked of Mackenzie. 'Need a ride, do you?'

'No, tha——'

'I don't think you quite understood what I said,' Neile broke in crossly. 'I have just told you that I'm being kidnapped!'

'So you have.' Grinning at her, he walked back round to the driver's seat and climbed unconcernedly in. Opening his paper on the wheel, he proceeded to read it.

'Well, aren't you going to do anything about it?' she demanded incredulously.

'No, love, not on a Friday.'

'Piqued, repiqued and repotted, or whatever the expression is. Come along, Neile, might as well give in gracefully.'

Grasping her arm, he helped her none too gently towards his car, which was now parked tidily to one side.

'You're the most——'

'I know,' he broke in gently. His eyes full of teasing laughter, he added, tongue in cheek. 'It's probably an Arien trait.'

'Oh, shut up. Did you really leave your car with the door open?'

'Yes. I really did. In you go.'

With a defeated sigh, she climbed in and was driven swiftly back to his house. Which is what you wanted all along, isn't it, Neile? she said to herself.

The housekeeper looked chagrined; Daniel delighted; and Mackenzie? Peeping sideways at him, she found him doing the same to her and her lips twitched before she hastily straightened them.

'You enjoy it, don't you?' he asked softly. 'Fighting with me. Don't you, Neile?'

Her lips pursed, she gave a reluctant nod.

'Never found anyone to play with before who was up to your weight? Is that it?'

'Perhaps.' Yet it was true in a way. People didn't fight with her, they gave in, and where was the fun in that? But to enjoy arguing, that must make her some sort of oddity, mustn't it? Yet she didn't really want to argue with anyone else. Normally, she was the peacemaker—well, mostly, she qualified to herself. It was only men and their lewd suggestions that drove her into a fury. But, with Mackenzie, she seemed to want to argue about anything and everything. Why? Needing to fight fire with fire? Whatever the reason, it seemed to give life a great deal of spice. She liked him, felt comfortable with him; had been fascinated by him from the moment they'd met. Even his stubbornness in not believing her didn't make her hate him. And it should, she thought defeatedly. She should hate him, really she should. Heaving a big sigh, she allowed him to arrange her comfortably on the sofa, a cushion beneath her injured foot.

'Right,' he said briskly. 'David first.'

'What?'

Without answering, he went to the door and shouted for David.

'You're not going to ask him now?' she asked, horrified. 'Not in front of me?'

'That's precisely what I'm going to do. No more pussy-footing around, Neile. All cards on the table. Ah, David. . .'

With a groan of embarrassment, Neile turned her face into the cushion and shut her ears to the inquisition until Mackenzie demanded, 'Well, Neile, believe him?'

Oh, God. Turning back, she glanced awkwardly at David, who was looking totally nonplussed. 'I don't know, do I?' she exclaimed fretfully. 'I wasn't listening—anyway, I told you I couldn't be sure.'

'All right, David,' Mackenzie said quietly, his gaze fixed firmly on Neile. 'Get the car out, will you?'

With a nod, he left.

'You really are a sod, you know. The poor man looked totally mortified.'

'He also looked innocent, don't you think? Well?'

'Yes,' she admitted grudgingly.

'Right, I'm now going to see Caroline——'

'Well, I'm not coming with you!' she declared forcefully.

'I didn't ask you to. And don't leave while I'm away. I'll be back tomorrow.'

'Dictator,' she scolded, only she was talking to an empty room. She then had to endure Mrs Needham's embarrassment. She came in looking as though she were going bravely to the scaffold. 'If you've come to give me a hard time, don't,' Neile said rudely. 'I already feel as though I've been through a shredder.'

'I came to apologise,' she said with quiet dignity.

'Well, don't do that either. It wasn't your fault I was dumped in your lap! God, that man is so arrogant!' she burst out. When Mrs Needham neither moved nor spoke, she looked at her and gave an apologetic grimace. 'Sorry, I'm behaving like a child—but these past few days have not been easy! Why can't I just go home?'

'Oh, gawd,' Mrs Needham exclaimed comically.

Staring at her in astonishment, Neile gave a snort of laughter. 'I couldn't have put it better myself.' Watching her curiously, she asked, 'Did you know Caroline?'

'Oh, yes,' she said feelingly.

'And didn't like her?'

'No, I didn't like her.'

She obviously wasn't going to elaborate, for which Neile couldn't really blame her. With a deep sigh, she leaned back. 'So now we wait. She'll lie, you know she'll lie, don't you?'

'Of course she will,' Ned said briskly. 'She always does! Never mind her, you haven't had any lunch and it's now nearly teatime. I've also to go into town to get you some clothes. You can't keep wearing those.'

'No,' Neile agreed gloomily. 'I probably smell.'

Staring at her uninvited guest, Mrs Needham burst out laughing, then shook her head. 'If you jot down your sizes I'll go and get you some jeans or something, a sweater, underwear. I'll get you something to eat first. . .'

'You can't go now! It's dark, and the shops will be shut soon. Tomorrow will do, surely?'

'All right, that would be easier. Now, I'll go and give Daniel his tea and get you something.'

'Where is he, by the way?'

'Up in his room. He's making a model or something or other; he's a solitary little chap.' With a last smile, Mrs Needham bustled back to the kitchen.

After Daniel had gone to bed, Neile spent the evening staring blindly at the television, and at nine-thirty decided she'd had enough. As days went, this one couldn't by any stretch of the imagination have been called a success.

Mackenzie returned late the following afternoon, and strode into the lounge where she was idly leafing through a magazine. Looking up, she tossed the magazine aside, and, not being one to wait calmly for the axe to fall, demanded, 'Well?' When he didn't answer, merely came to stand in front of her looking tired and harassed, she added, 'That bad, huh? What did darling Caroline have to say?'

'Not much.' Sliding his hand into his pocket, he withdrew a Polaroid photograph. He held it out to her, and asked quietly, 'Is that the man you saw?'

Glancing at it, then taking it and looking more closely, she nodded. It showed the fair-haired man quite clearly, taken from a distance of about twenty feet. He had his head turned towards the camera, his face wearing a startled expression as though he'd been taken by surprise. Having now met David, she could clearly see the difference between the two men. 'Yes, that's him,' she agreed. 'He was at Caroline's?'

'Yes.'

'And?'

Sighing, he took the photo back and put it absently in his pocket. 'And you were right,' he admitted quietly, his eyes almost unfocused as he stared down at her. 'His name's Harrison, by the way. He followed us after we'd dropped Daniel off.'

'Then why didn't we see him when we ran out of petrol?' she asked, puzzled.

'Because we were on the wrong road,' he explained tiredly, 'and he knew very well that that road didn't go anywhere. All he had to do was wait at the crossroads until we came back. When we hadn't returned by midnight, he drove down the lane until he saw the empty car. Assuming that we'd found somewhere to stay, he drove back to the crossroads and presumably spent the night in his car. He picked us up the following morning after we'd been to the garage, and then down to Sussex.'

'And followed me to work the next morning?'

'No, easier than that. He asked in the village shop who the exquisite young lady was who lived he thought in the old cottage in Mill Lane. The shopkeeper was delighted to tell him all about you and your mother. He even told him the name of your agency, where it was, what you did.' With a faint smile, he continued, 'Ellen obviously gives the whole village chapter and verse about her daughter's affairs. Harrison then returned to Yorkshire and it was a simple matter to drive down the lane where we'd got lost and ask around about his friend who was touring the district. Mrs Goff was apparently very helpful,' he concluded flatly.

'I see. Well, I'm glad it's all been sorted out.'

'Yes.' Still staring down at her, his face empty, he

added quietly and with bitter self-recrimination, 'I don't come out of it very well, do I?'

Not knowing how to answer, she looked away.

'Not only do I judge you guilty without the least vestige of proof, I won't listen when you try to explain. I abuse you physically; abduct you—well, there's not much I haven't done, is there? And then, with every reason to despise me, you take the trouble to explain to my son that his father loves him. And then—then,' he continued harshly, 'not satisfied with all that, I compound my stupidity by accusing you of——'

'Mackenzie, don't,' she interrupted, unable to take any more. 'It's over. Let it lie.'

Twisting away from her, he went to stand before the fire, his arms along the mantelshelf. 'I can't,' he exclaimed, his voice muffled.

Staring at his bowed back, she asked quietly, 'So who was Harrison?'

'Her current man-friend.'

Not totally sure about the wisdom in asking, but nevertheless needing to know, she asked carefully, 'Does it bother you? Harrison being her—er—friend?'

Turning his head, he regarded her with a puzzled frown. 'Bother me? In what way?'

Looking down, she explained quietly, 'I thought perhaps you might mind—because you were still a bit in love with her,' she concluded in a little rush.

'In love with Caroline? Good God, no! I fell out of love with her years ago! Whatever made you think I might be?'

'Oh, I don't know,' she denied lamely, 'but, if she knew you didn't love her, was that why she went through all that to try and prove you an unfit father?'

'Yes, she was trying to hurt me, make me suffer. . .'

'But that would make her son suffer too,' she exclaimed, perplexed. 'No one surely, no matter how warped their nature, would deliberately try to hurt their own son.'

'I don't think it was deliberate, not directed at Daniel anyway. He just happened to be in the middle, but if she could turn him against me, make him think I didn't love him, then that would hurt me. I don't think it even occurred to her that it would hurt Daniel even more.'

'I thought perhaps she was trying to get you back. . .'

'Back? No, she knew there was no chance of that. No. I fell out of love with her, you see, so I had to be punished.' Straightening, he turned to face her and rested his shoulders against the mantelpiece instead. 'When we were first married, I thought she was the most wonderful person in the whole wide world. I thought her generous, happy, even-tempered. She was none of those things, only for a long time I wouldn't admit it to myself. Told myself her increasing petulance was my fault because I was busy so often, trying to make a go of my career.' Staring at her, not really seeing her, he continued reflectively, 'Caroline needs adulation, to be seen, admired, flirted with. Mostly in those early years of our marriage I didn't have the time, or to be honest the energy for partying every night, going out to dinner. Gradually, inevitably, there was more resentment than affection, so she started trying to make me jealous. When I saw what was happening, I blamed myself, tried to spend more time with her, and for a while everything was fine. Only inevitably there were business trips, meetings I had to attend. She should really have married someone who was already wealthy, who didn't need to work, who could give her the attention she needed. She was spoilt, you see; I knew that, but in my arrogance I assumed love would conquer all. Only of course it doesn't.

'After a while, I suppose I gave up trying—only perversely, once she saw that, she seemed determined to make a go of it, and because I felt guilty, because I hadn't given her the attention she needed, I agreed. We decided to start a family; she said a child would make her more contented.'

'Only of course it didn't,' Neile said sympathetically.

'No, of course it didn't, and it was a damned criminal thing to do, to bring a child into the world in those circumstances. She had a bad pregnancy and I think felt nothing for the child before he was even born. Perhaps she also assumed that once born he would lie tidily in his cot, look adorable, that she would show him off and everyone would admire him and her.'

'Only of course babies cry, are sick. . .'

'Yes, and Daniel seemed to cry rather a lot.'

'Because he knew, because he felt unwanted by his mother. . .'

'Perhaps. Yes, probably.'

'Not probably! Definitely!' she said more shortly than she intended and he looked at her sharply.

'Yes,' he admitted. 'You're right, of course you are, so there was more guilt. And then, when Daniel soon became the most important thing in my world, Caroline hated me for it. Because I gave to Daniel what I could no longer give to her.'

'And she's been making you pay for it ever since.'

'Mmm.'

'And you thought I was like her.'

'Yes, Neile, I thought you were like her.'

'Because of the way I look.'

'Yes. On one level I could like you. You made me laugh; you made me angry, frustrated and confused. I couldn't believe that someone who looked like you couldn't be mercenary, selfish. Yet you began the agency, struggled to make a go of something that on the surface looked only worth writing off, and I had a reluctant admiration for your—oh, bloody-mindedness, I suppose. You're irreverent, aggressive, diff——'

'I'm only aggressive with you,' she pointed out with slight tartness, as though it was important to have the point clarified.

With a faint smile, he continued, 'Difficult—and

lovable. And without effort you made Daniel love you, and I think I hated you for that.'

'But why?' she asked in confusion.

'Because I was jealous,' he admitted quietly. Turning towards her, he added scathingly, 'See what a nice character I have?'

'But jealous of what?'

'Of your ability to communicate with my son. Ever since the divorce was finalised and I got custody, there's been a barrier between us, and I didn't know why, and when I saw him cuddled up on the bed with you, Daniel looking content, happy, I was jealous. Ever since the first time you met, he's talked about you as though there was some sort of bond that excluded me.'

'I can't imagine why; I barely said two words to him and he certainly didn't chatter away to me. In fact most of the time I felt totally inadequate. I don't know very much about children, what to say to them. . .'

'It wasn't so much what you said, I think, but the fact that he obviously felt safe with you, comfortable—oh, hell, Neile, I don't know,' he muttered helplessly. 'I only know that when I saw him on the bed with you, looking trusting and almost loving, I hated you. Whenever I picked him up, held him, he'd sit rigidly, stiff, and I didn't know what to do about it. I only heard part of your words to him, registered only part, the bit about being bought, and I just—exploded.'

'I wasn't trying to be interfering or anything,' she explained weakly, 'only to try and make things right. It seemed important that I be truthful. . .'

'Do you think I don't know that now?' he exclaimed. 'Lord, Neile, when I read your note, I—oh, God, I don't know. I think I went a little crazy. I chased after you—and—well, you know the rest.' Raking his untidy hair back, he gave a twisted smile. 'Ever since I met you, my life has lurched from one disaster to another.' Walking across to her, he perched on the sofa beside her. 'You drive me insane, you know that, don't you?

You goad me, Neile Markham. Dear lord, but how you goad me.'

'Not on purpose. . .'

'Don't you? It sometimes seems that way—and I have to confess there's an element of ruthless prodding on my side; you always rise so beautifully. So now I have to try and make it up to you,' he concluded quietly.

'No, you don't.'

'Yes, Neile, I do.'

CHAPTER NINE

ARGUE as Neile might, Mackenzie refused to listen. He was determined to make amends, and amends he was going to make whether she wanted him to or not.

'I've already arranged it,' he said smoothly. 'David is at this moment taking Thelma's car back to her. He will then collect your things from the office, collect your car, drive with Thelma to your flat, where she will pack you up some clothes and give them to David. He will drive down to Sussex, give your case to Ellen and return here. Meanwhile—meanwhile,' he continued firmly when she tried to get a word in edgeways, 'I will be driving you down. So, while I shower and change, you will go upstairs, collect up anything you have, and then we will leave.'

'There is no need——'

'There is every need,' he replied with quiet determination.

Taking a deep breath, she levered herself upright, faced him squarely, or as squarely as she could standing on only one leg, and promptly overbalanced on to the coffee-table. In trying to save herself she knocked over the teacup and it crashed to the floor and shattered.

'Damn.'

'Quite. Well done, Neile,' he said drily.

'Sorry,' she muttered perfunctorily, 'but it's your own fault. You ride roughshod—treat me as though I have a terminal illness. . .'

With a wide smile, he bent down to pick up the broken china. 'Why is it, I wonder, that everything you do is my fault?' Still crouched, the china cradled in his hands, he watched her thoughtfully for a moment. 'Come and spend Christmas with us. . .'

'No, I've already made arrangements to spend it with Ellen.'

'Bring Ellen with you——'

'I don't want to bring Ellen with me!'

'Then come up for New Year. Please?'

Knowing she needed to have it spelled out, she asked bluntly, 'Why?'

'So that we can get to know each other properly, without all the hassle and aggression that's been going on between us. In between hating you, I liked you, and I suppose I need to find out if my feelings are only generated by anger and mistrust. I don't know, Neile,' he confessed. 'Can't we take it a step at a time? Your feelings for me aren't entirely of dislike, are they?'

'No, you know very well they aren't. Although what the hell they are, the lord alone knows.'

With another faint smile, he went on, 'So will you? Come up and stay for a while? Will you be generous enough? You once asked me to be magnanimous; now I'm asking it of you.'

Staring at him, she sighed long and deeply, 'I'll think about it.'

'Thank you.' Looking away from her, he finished picking up the broken pieces then stood. 'It's a mess, isn't it?'

'I'm sorry, I'll replace it——'

'I didn't mean the china,' he said, exasperated. 'I meant us. Too much has happened too quickly until neither of us can see straight.'

'Yes,' she agreed weakly.

'So I think we need to spend some time just relaxing, being ordinary.'

'Ordinary?' she echoed on a small laugh. 'I doubt you've ever been ordinary in your life!'

'Well, certainly not since I met you, no. Go and get packed up.' The smile still hovering around his mouth, he took the broken china out to the kitchen.

Give in, Neile, you might just as well. With a wry smile, she limped upstairs to collect her things.

She was rather surprised to find that Mackenzie had changed into a suit. It seemed a bit formal just to drive her to Sussex. Perhaps he had a business meeting somewhere afterwards. Settling herself in the car, she relaxed back and allowed herself to be driven.

Two hours later Mackenzie was pulling in to the kerb outside Ellen's cottage. Neile's car, which David had been driving, was already parked.

'He made good time,' she commented inanely.

'Mmm.'

With a little chuckle, she unlatched her door, only to have Mackenzie reach across and pull it to again.

His face of necessity close to hers, he said quietly. 'I'll come and let you out.'

Staring into eyes that were so very close, she swallowed hard, then looked quickly down.

'*Déjà vu*, Neile?' he asked softly. 'I vividly recall another time, another journey. . .'

'Yes.' Remembering something that had puzzled her, she asked, 'Why were you so abrupt that day? I mean, you'd been nice to me up until then, but suddenly you changed.'

'Didn't you realise?' he asked gently. 'Kissing you, holding you, wanting you, I suddenly realised how selfish I was being. My life was in one hell of a mess; hardly fair to ask you to wait until I'd sorted it out. So I decided it would be best to finish it. Only this time—we'll do it differently, hmm?'

'Yes,' she whispered hoarsely.

'And, this time, perhaps we can get it right.'

Blushing faintly, she waited for him to get out and walk round to release her. Did he mean, get it right to become friends? Or more?

Taking her arm and slamming the car door, he helped her up the path.

'Don't do things by halves, do you?' was Ellen's only comment to her daughter as she opened the front door. It was Mackenzie who got the welcoming kiss.

'It's my charm,' he said to Neile *sotto voce*.

'No, it isn't,' she denied, 'Ellen just likes younger men.'

With a little laugh, he closed the front door.

'Your man's in the kitchen,' Ellen tossed over her shoulder as she led the way along the hall, 'having a cup of tea.'

Feeling nervous for no very good reason that she could think of, Neile sat at the kitchen table opposite the chauffeur. Giving him a smile, she said quietly, 'Thank you for collecting my things. I seem to have been a lot of trouble to everyone.'

'You've always been a lot of trouble,' Ellen commented. Then, with a wide smile, she bent and gave Neile a hug. 'It's lovely to see you. Sit down, Mackenzie, have a cup of tea. Neile—upstairs,' she ordered. 'You need to shower and change.' With a wink at Mackenzie, she urged her daughter up and back into the hall.

'Why do I need to shower and change?'

'Because I said so. Come on, up with you.'

'And you call me bossy?' Neile complained as she hopped upstairs to her room. Collapsing on to the side of the bed, she regarded her mother with her head on one side. 'So, how are you?'

'Me?' Ellen exclaimed comically. 'Me? You're the one who's been causing all the trouble!' Plumping down beside her daughter, a twinkle in her blue eyes, she asked, 'So, how have you been getting on with him?'

'With who?' Neile asked innocently.

'Don't play smart with me, miss—Mackenzie, of course!'

'Didn't he tell you?' Neile hedged.

'Some,' she admitted unhelpfully. 'I did warn you, didn't I? You can't push Ariens, you have to lead them. And you want to, darling, don't you?' she added softly.

With a despairing little sigh, she nodded. 'Yes,' she agreed, 'I want to. Do you like him?'

'Yes, I do, very much. He's attractive without being conceited, strong without being overpowering——'

'Much you know,' Neile put in with a rueful smile.

'He won't give a damn what anybody thinks—except for the woman he falls in love with.'

'Is that an oblique reference to Gordon?'

'Perhaps. He wasn't strong. He was never right for you, darling.'

'And you think Mackenzie is?'

'Only you can really know that, but, from an outsider's point of view, yes, I think he could be right for you.'

'But I argue with him,' she exclaimed despairingly. 'Librans aren't supposed to argue!'

'Not as a general rule of thumb, no; traditionally, they're peacemakers, but when dealing with someone as strong as Mackenzie it's necessary to keep the balance by matching his temperament. Keeping the scales equal—that's the true Libran's role.'

'Do you really believe all that?' Neile asked wistfully.

'Of course I do! And Libra and Aries are among the most compatible signs. Fire and air. Now, come along and have your shower; Mackenzie's booked a table at Middleton's for eight-thirty——'

'What?'

'Eight-thirty. He's taking you out to dinner.'

'He never said——'

'Yes, he did. To me.' Ellen grinned. 'Wear your black dress. Have you ever been there?' When Neile weakly shook her head, she explained with a smile, 'Very exclusive, not to say posh, so make yourself look nice. Pity about that bandage—oh, well.'

Left alone, Neile slumped tiredly, prey to all sorts of conflicting emotions, until her mother's voice echoed along the landing.

'Neile? I can't hear that shower!'

Pulling a little face, she levered herself up and went into the bathroom.

Standing before the mirror half an hour later, she was astonished to find that her stomach was full of butterflies. Ridiculous. Checking her watch, she saw that it was almost eight o'clock; no time to linger further, she would have to do. With a final blot to her coral lipstick, she gave herself a last overall appraisal. Pity about the wretched bandage. Flat shoes were going to look horrendous. So why wear them? Why indeed. Defiantly taking high-heeled ones from her wardrobe, she sat on the bed and slipped on the left one. Holding the right one in her hand and eyeing the slim, very slim elegance of it, she stared down at her bandaged ankle. It's not going to fit, Neile, so don't even attempt it. No.

'Neile?'

'Just coming,' she answered hastily. Removing the shoe she had on, she got to her feet and limped out to the landing. Mackenzie was waiting at the foot of the stairs and she halted uncertainly.

It seemed a very long time that he stood and stared up at her, his expression unreadable, before he asked quietly, 'Can you manage?'

'Yes,' she whispered huskily. Grasping the banister in one hand, her shoe in the other, she hopped slowly down, then halted uncertainly on the bottom step.

'You look lovely,' he approved, his voice ever so slightly husky.

'Thank you.'

With a tiny smile, a faint light of humour in his eyes, he commented softly, 'Good girl.'

'What does that mean?'

'It means that I expected to be told that being lovely wasn't everything, and that you would rather be admired for your fine mind. Am I allowed to admire both?' he teased.

With a jerky little nod, and needing desperately to change the subject, she held out her shoe.

'You want me to play Prince Charming?'

'No! I mean, I didn't—I just meant I wasn't sure whether to wear it,' she concluded lamely.

'Of course you must wear it.' Holding her eyes, he reached to the side of the newel post and produced a pair of crutches.

'Where on earth did you get those?'

'I didn't. Ellen has been playing fairy godmother.'

'It's not all she's been playing by the sound of it. Nor you either. I feel like the object of a conspiracy.'

'And so you are.' He grinned. 'Come on, try these on for size.'

Hopping down to the hall, she took the crutches and put them beneath her arms. As soon as she was balanced, Mackenzie bent down and eased her good foot into her shoe. Whether it was deliberate or not, she didn't know, but his hand lingered for a few seconds on her slim ankle, and she gave a little shiver of awareness. 'There,' he said softly as he straightened. 'Ellen? We're off now.'

Bustling out from the kitchen, Ellen draped a beautiful woollen cloak round Neile's shoulders. 'Early Christmas present,' she whispered. Standing on tiptoe, she hugged her daughter warmly and pressed a kiss to her cheek. 'You look lovely, darling, have a wonderful time.'

Her eyes prickling with tears at such an unusual demonstration of affection, she squeezed her mother's hand. 'Thank you, it's lovely.'

'And goes just right with your black dress.' Turning to Mackenzie, she smiled softly at him. 'Take care of her, won't you?'

'Yes, Ellen. I'll take very great care of her.' And, extraordinarily, he sounded slightly emotional himself. 'Sure you won't change your mind?' he asked her, and when she shook her head he did something even more extraordinary. He picked her up in a bear-hug, and pressed a warm kiss on her cheek.

'What was that all about?' Neile asked him when he'd settled her in the car.

'What was what all about?'

'Mackenzie! About Mother changing her mind. Changing it about what?'

'Joining us for dinner, of course.'

'Oh.' Still slightly puzzled by the exchange in the hall, she absently stroked her hand down the front of the cloak. 'It's beautiful, isn't it?'

'Yes, Neile, it is. A beautiful cloak for a beautiful lady.'

The restaurant was every bit as exclusive as Ellen had said. It wasn't very large, only a dozen or so tables, each sitting in its own little pool of light. A waiter discreetly disposed of her crutches and wrap, smiled at her, conferred with Mackenzie, and gradually her taut nerves relaxed. By the time she had eaten her way through three courses, drunk heaven alone knew how many glasses of wine, she was feeling distinctly mellow and happy. Gazing across the candlelit table at her companion, she gave him a beautiful smile. She didn't see his caught breath, or the ever so slightly clenched hand on his own wine glass, only saw how devastatingly attractive he was. I love you, she told him silently. I don't know how or why it happened, just that it did, and if you send me away now, or we can't resolve our differences, I think it will break my heart.

'What are you thinking?' he asked quietly.

Shaking her head, she took another sip of her wine. 'It's been a lovely evening, thank you.'

'Thank you,' he returned, and toasting her with his glass he added, 'May it be the first of many.'

A lovely warm glow inside, she agreed.

'Ready to go home?' he asked in the same soft, gentle voice.

'Yes.'

Summoning the waiter with a little gesture that probably only worked for the very few, he settled the bill while another waiter brought her her crutches and cloak.

The crisp night air, instead of clearing her head, only

made her sleepy. With a contented sigh, she relaxed into the soft upholstery of the car and closed her eyes.

The well-bred purr of the engine, the smooth rhythm of the wheels on the road, lulled her into sleep. A gentle finger touching her cheek woke her, and she opened her eyes. Mackenzie was watching her, and she gave a slow, contented smile.

'Are we home?'

'Yes.'

Something in his voice, a slight tension, made her frown and look at him properly. 'Is something wrong?'

His eyes held hers almost interrogatively for endless moments before he shook his head. 'I hope not.' With a little movement of his head, he indicated for her to look through the windscreen.

Doing so, she saw not Ellen's cottage but a house covered with ivy. 'But that's. . .'

'Yes. My home.'

Struggling to find comprehension, she turned to look back at him. 'But why? Why are we here?'

'Because I want you here. Because I want you to spend Christmas with us.'

'But I told you I was spending it with Ellen! She's expecting me!'

'No, she isn't,' he denied quietly.

'What?'

'I said she isn't expecting you. As soon as we left the cottage, David was going to run her down to her sister in Eastbourne. I asked her to spend it up here, but she said it would be better for her to go to her sister.'

'She knew you intended to bring me up here?'

'Yes.'

Remembering back to the little scene in the hall when Ellen had given her the cloak, she accused, 'That was why you asked her if she'd changed her mind.'

'Yes.'

'But why did no one tell me? Why couldn't you have just asked?'

'Because I didn't think you would come,' he said simply.

Feeling helpless, she exclaimed lamely, 'But you can't just make arrangements without asking! Supposing I hadn't fallen asleep?'

'I don't know. I'd have thought of something else, I expect.'

'You don't even look—ashamed,' she moaned. 'Oh, Mackenzie, I wish you hadn't done this. . .'

'Why?'

'Why?' she exclaimed. 'Why?'

'Yes,' he persisted. 'Why?'

Staring at him, into the light silver eyes, she burst out in exasperation, 'I don't know, do I? I want to go home!'

'Stop being difficult.'

When he moved away, opened his door and climbed out, she stared after him in astonishment. Difficult? He was the one being difficult!

Watching him as he walked round to her side, she sighed. She wasn't sure she was quite ready for this. She'd got it into her head that she wouldn't see him for a while; that she would have time to think about him in peace; and now he was giving her no time at all.

When he unlatched her door, and then leaned in to help her out, she caught the faint scent of his aftershave. Spicy, familiar, stomach-churningly heady, and suddenly every breath he took, every movement, seemed magnified, larger than life, and she wanted desperately to touch him, have him touch her, take away the uncertainty she was feeling.

'Is it such a terrible thing to have done?' he asked quietly. 'To want you with me? To want to get to know you?'

'No,' she whispered.

'Then what's wrong?'

'I don't know,' she confessed confusedly. 'I think I'm nervous.'

'Oh, good,' he said with a faint smile as he helped her out and took her arm, 'because I'm bloody terrified.'

She didn't believe that, but before she could comment the front door opened and Ned ushered them quickly inside. 'Come on, hurry up, you're letting all the cold in.'

'Sorry,' Mackenzie apologised with a little grimace. 'And I thought I told you not to wait up?'

'So you did.' She smiled. 'David got back a few minutes ago. He's put Miss Markham's case in her room, and now he's gone off to spend the holiday with his sister and her family. All right? He said you knew all about it.'

'Yes, thanks.' Ushering Neile into the lounge, a lounge that had been transformed in her absence, he removed her cloak and urged, 'Sit down, rest your ankle, I'll go and arrange for some coffee.' Barely waiting for her to acknowledge his words, he hurried out and closed the door.

Confused and made uncertain by his change from charming escort to abrupt host, she perched on the edge of the sofa and stared round her at the decorations that now brightened the long room. A large Christmas tree stood at one end, a rather bedraggled star sitting drunkenly on the top, and she smiled. Daniel's handiwork, no doubt.

She turned her head as the door opened to admit Mackenzie, and her smile died. 'The room looks nice,' she commented inanely.

'Yes, Daniel insisted it had to be done before you came back.'

'You told him? But supposing I hadn't come? That's what I find so irritating,' she continued pettishly, 'your certainty that I can so easily be manipulated.'

'Certainty?' he asked in astonishment. 'I had about as much certainty as a baby bird being hurled from the nest on his first flying lesson!'

'Don't be ridiculous!' Eyeing his large frame, she gave a snort of laughter.

With a faint smile, which didn't seem to carry much conviction, he walked across to the fire. 'Ankle OK?'

'It's fine. Getting better all the time. How's your hand? I never did remember to ask you.'

'It's also fine—Neile, this is ridiculous!'

'Yes.' Peeping at him sideways, she gave a little giggle that owed more to nerves than humour. 'Well, it's your own fault, you shouldn't have hijacked me, and, before you ask, yes, I am warm enough, no, I am not tired; I don't have a headache——'

'Shut up,' he said softly, his eyes full of rueful amusement. Straightening, he began again, only to sigh crossly as Ned came in with a tray. 'Thank you, Ned. Now go away. Go to bed or something.'

'Yes, sir,' she said, her face creased with humour. 'Welcome back, Miss Markham, it's nice to see you again.'

'Thanks, Ned. I'll let you know if it's nice to *be* back tomorrow.'

As Ned went out with a chuckle, Mackenzie gave her a pained look. 'That was uncalled for.'

'I know, but if we don't get the conversation going soon I'm going to have hysterics.'

'Yes, well, I don't find this easy.' Moving across to the couch, he pulled the coffee-table towards him so that he could reach to pour out. Handing her a cup, he then spent an inordinate amount of time pouring out his own.

Examining his face, which gave so little of his thoughts away as he stirred in sugar, the thick lashes that were lowered to hide his eyes, she found it was almost more than she could bear not to reach out, touch him. His hair needed cutting, she noticed; it was beginning to curl over his collar and she wanted to run her finger along the back of his neck, tidy it. 'What did you buy Daniel for Christmas?' she asked quietly.

'Oh, don't start that again,' he muttered, sounding impatient and irritable. 'I need to talk to you.'

'Then talk.'

'I'm trying to, dammit! I had it all worked out, you know, what I was going to say, when you complained at my high-handedness. . .'

'I might not have done. . .'

With a rude snort, he continued, 'How I was going to behave. . .' Looking at her from the corner of his eye, he gave the muffled grunt of laughter that she always found so endearing. 'I was going to be gentle, ordinary——'

'You've never been ordinary in your life!' she put in.

'Ordinary,' he repeated. 'Treat you like my sister. . .'

'Do you have a sister? I didn't know that——'

'Neile! No, I don't have a sister. I was using it as an example—and stop laughing at me!'

'Sorry,' she apologised, her eyes full of amusement.

'I'm making a real hash of this, aren't I?' he asked ruefully. 'I was going to lead up to it gradually, try to find out how you felt about me—only I can't,' he exclaimed almost in despair. 'I can't. I sat and watched you in that restaurant, saw the looks thrown at you, the smiles the waiter gave, and I kept remembering how it felt, how you felt, and it's driving me insane! I can't be near you without wanting to grab you, hold you, feel your mouth under mine, and I cannot sit here making inane conversation about—trivia! These last few hours have seemed like a lifetime! I haven't been able to stop thinking about you. Thinking about making love to you until I began to wonder if I was quite normal! Supposing I was like one of those men you read about in the newspapers? God, you have no idea what I've been going through.'

'Oh, but I have,' she said softly as she put her cup down with a hand that shook.

'I don't even know you! Have you any idea how many times—what? What did you just say?'

'I said I have,' she repeated shakily.

'You have?'

'Yes. I wasn't going to get involved with anyone ever again. I'd promised myself that. After Gordon——'

'Gordon?' he asked stupidly.

'Yes, Gordon. He hurt me very badly. He couldn't handle it, you see, other men making remarks, asking him how good I was in bed, making crude suggestions as though because I looked the way I did that I was different, like some erotic specialist. And I'm not like that. I'm ordinary. Inside, I'm so ordinary, you wouldn't believe. . .'

'No, you aren't,' he denied thickly.

'Yes, I am. So he left. Just packed up and left. Goodbye, Neile; sorry, I can't hack it. . . I thought he loved me. So I promised myself, no more, and then I met you. You annoyed me, irritated me, made me lose my temper—and I wanted you to make love to me. And you never did. I find it hard to believe that I barely know you. . .'

'Do you still want me to make love to you?' he asked, his voice an uneven thread of sound.

'Yes.'

'Now?'

'Yes.'

'It's not the wine talking?'

'No.'

They stared at each other, their faces so close, almost touching, their eyes dark, watching, and she never knew who moved first, Mackenzie or herself, only knew that suddenly they were in each other's arms and his mouth was covering hers warmly, urgently, with a desperate kind of longing. Her fingers clenched in his jacket, she arched towards him, her breathing out of control. She held him as tight as he was holding her, and they exchanged hungry, passionate kisses until she thought her heart would burst with wanting him. It was no longer enough just to be close and her hands slid with rough insistence to undo his shirt-buttons. Impatiently wrenching the material aside, she caught her breath as her palms encountered warm skin and she splayed her fingers wide holding him, needing him, wanting him inside her, belonging to her, even if only for that one moment in time.

It didn't seem a conscious thought to undress, it just happened. They stood, their mouths still fused, and shrugged out of their clothes. Neither was gentle. She didn't want his gentleness, nor he hers. From standing, suddenly they were lying, the fire hot along her side, his mouth hot and demanding on hers, his arms tense, crushing her body with a warm, smothering blanket that burned her far more than any flame. When his mouth slid to her throat, his voice was muffled and uneven as he told her things she didn't hear, whispered her name over and over, and she gave herself up to the pleasure and the pain of loving him. Whatever he wanted would be his, whatever he wanted her to be, she would be, for this one special moment she belonged entirely to this man whom she didn't think she could live without.

Meeting him movement for movement, her breath held as she strained to match his rhythm, she cried out as he shuddered, halted, brought them both to fulfilment, then, with a long, shuddering sigh that was echoed in her heart, breathing was easier, living was just possible. Dragging breath into her aching lungs, she lay, holding him, his head resting against hers, his body still, content.

'The little death, isn't that what the French call it?' she asked shakily when her heart had regained some of its normal rhythm. '*La petite mort.* Now I know why.'

Smoothing her palms along his back, his shoulders, spine, down to his waist, she sighed, a long slow sigh of pleasure and relief. It was almost like being liberated, all that angry passion unleashed. With a soft smile, she trailed gentle kisses along his shoulder, revelling in the taste and texture of his skin, the sheer animal warmth of him. She didn't want to move, just lie like this, holding him. 'Are you asleep, my man?' she asked with a little gurgle of laughter.

'Mmm,' he mumbled as he slowly stirred, moved his head so that he could look down into her face. Supporting his weight on his forearms he stared down into her eyes—and slowly smiled. 'Ordinary?' he queried with a trace of his old mockery.

Her own mouth curving in response, she lightly kissed his nose.

His eyes crinkling at the corners, he did the same for her. 'I don't believe,' he said softly, 'that I had any right to experience that. Not with you, not ever, not after all the things I did to you.'

'I think that's how it's supposed to be,' she said dreamily. 'Perhaps that's how it always is, for others.'

'No,' he denied. 'I don't think so—no, I'm bloody sure so!' he exclaimed. 'I'm no novice, Neile, but I have never in my entire life experienced that. Not with anyone. Ever! So it looks as though I will have to move back to London, doesn't it? Because whatever say you have in anything, I am not letting you go! I think I'm going to be insatiable.' His mouth moving with slow enjoyment, he tasted the warm flesh of her throat, then down to the creamy curves of her breasts.

'Why can't I just move up here with you?' she breathed shakily as she suddenly found her lungs unable to cope with the ill treatment she was giving them. 'Surely that would be easier?' she gasped, then tensed, her muscles locking as he roved lower, his tongue trailing fire across her stomach. 'Oh, Mackenzie, no. . .'

'Oh, Mackenzie, yes,' he contradicted with a little chuckle.

'You're robbing me of concentration. . .'

'Good.'

'Oh,' she groaned as he moved yet lower, then gasped in surprise. 'Oh. . .'

Shaking with laughter, he reluctantly abandoned his

exploration and returned to look down into her face. 'Didn't you like it?'

'Well, yes,' she murmured, her face pink. 'It was just a bit—um—unexpected.'

'You've been reading the wrong books, my love.'

'Obviously!'

With a gentle smile, he framed her hot face with his large palms. 'Did I tell you how adorable you are?'

'No. At least, I don't think so.'

'Then I'll tell you now. You are one very adorable lady. Now, what were you trying to tell me?'

'I haven't the faintest idea,' she confessed. 'You made me forget—no, you didn't. I've just remembered. I was saying I could move up here with you. Come up Friday evening and go back Monday morning.'

His face suddenly serious, he asked quietly, 'And will just seeing me weekends satisfy you, Neile? Because they sure as hell won't satisfy me! I have no right to ask you to abandon the agency now when it's just beginning to do well, so, if the mountain won't—or can't—come to Muhammad, then Muhammad will have to go to the mountain. But would you really have moved up here if I'd asked you?'

'Yes,' she said simply. The agency now seemed rather a minor consideration. If it came to a choice, Mackenzie would win hands down. Yet before she could wholly commit herself, there were one or two things she desperately needed to know. She'd been hurt before; she couldn't bear for it to happen again.

'Mackenzie?'

'Mmm?'

'You know what I just said about Gordon? About how he couldn't handle other men?'

'I know,' he agreed quietly, 'and you are now wondering how I would handle it, yes?'

'Yes,' she whispered.

'To tell you the truth, Neile, I don't honestly know. I didn't handle myself very well in the hospital, did I, when those two goons practically fought over you? But that wasn't jealousy. . . No, don't stiffen and pull away, let me explain what I mean. I was fighting so hard to believe in you, in what you had said, and seeing those two—well, it was rather nastily reminiscent of the way Caroline used to behave.'

'But I didn't encourage them. . .'

'I know you didn't, but I was feeling particularly ragged just then. I hadn't expected to see you again when I returned from the States, and then to find you on my doorstep, and the ensuing argument—well, as I say, I wasn't thinking very rationally. But normally, if remarks are made, then I imagine that I would be angry, for your sake, that you should have to be subjected to such insults from small minds. I don't know what sort of friends Gordon had, but I can assure you that no friend of mine would ever speak slightingly of you, or to you. Neither in my presence, nor outside it. Other men genuinely admiring you—OK, that's one thing. Other men insulting you—I'd probably lynch them.'

'But it wouldn't affect you? Make you embarrassed?' she persisted.

'No.' Trailing a gentle finger down her cheek, he smiled. 'Angry, I suspect. And, if you looked at another man and smiled at him the way you smiled at me in the restaurant, insanely jealous; but not, I hope, possessively so without cause—that can destroy more easily than anything. I've seen it happen. Anything else? Yes, I can see there is,' he continued gently. 'Come on, ask.'

'All right.' Taking a deep breath, she plunged in, 'You said just now you weren't a novice. How much of a novice aren't you?' When he didn't immediately answer, she looked at him, her eyes worried.

'Are we back to Super Stud?' he asked slowly. 'You think there might be some truth in Caroline's accusations?'

'I don't know,' she confessed unhappily.

'Will you believe me if I tell you it isn't true?'

'Yes,' she admitted, because she suddenly realised it was necessary to trust him. 'The past I can handle—sort of,' she confessed with a funny little grimace, 'but I couldn't handle you going off with another woman. . .'

'Then I will tell you that, no, there is no truth in the accusations. There have been women, of course there have. After my marriage broke down, thcre was one. Not for long, but there was one. Since I met you, none.'

'Thank you. I had to ask. . .'

'I know. Neile? I work very hard, sometimes I have to go abroad. . .'

'I know,' she smiled, 'you said. I'm not Caroline, Mackenzie; I don't need parties, adulation; I'm a very quiet person usually—yes, I am,' she insisted when he looked sceptical. 'It's only with you that I behave in this quite extraordinary fashion. I shan't expect you to dance constant attendance on me.' I will try very hard not to expect anything, she mentally resolved, because if the only way to keep you is to be flexible, then I will be so flexible you wouldn't believe! But even if, against all her expectations, he fell in love with her, she wasn't the type of person to need to live in another's pocket, or to have them live in hers. She was the type of person who needed to be loved, and she just prayed that was what he was offering.

When he rolled on to his back, taking her with him, and settled her in the curve of his shoulder, she slid her hand with slow enjoyment across his chest. Feeling possessive, and afraid, and happy, she traced the shadows the flickering firelight made. 'Mackenzie?'

'Mmm?'

'If I had been guilty of all the things you thought, would you really have tried to destroy the agency?'

Turning his head so that his mouth grazed across her forehead, he sighed. 'I don't know. Probably not; vengeance has a nasty habit of turning and biting the avenger.' Shifting slightly, so that he could look down into her face, he smiled, a beautiful, warm, contented smile. 'Truth was, I didn't want you to be guilty. You'll never know how hard I fought to believe you; how many arguments I put forward, how many excuses.' Pushing his knee gently between her thighs, his smile turned wicked when she blushed.

'Don't do that,' she whispered without conviction, 'I can't think straight.'

'I don't want you to think straight,' he argued as he began to drop light, butterfly kisses across her face, 'because if you did, you might remember what a bastard I've been.'

'I do remember,' she said with a teasing smile that held just a tinge of sadness, 'and it doesn't matter. . .'

'Yes, it does, Neile,' he contradicted. 'It matters very much.' His face sobering, he moved into a sitting position and leaned back against the sofa. Pulling her up beside him, he continued quietly, 'I need you to understand so that you won't think it will ever happen again. If I hadn't liked you so much, if I hadn't had so many conflicting emotions going on inside me, I would never have behaved as I did. It was because I liked you, didn't want you to be what I——'

'I know that,' she put in gently. Lifting her hand, she turned his face towards her. 'Living with Caroline, from what I now know of her, would sour anyone's disposition.'

'Not so much of the sour, please,' he said with a grimace. 'There are enough accusations to level at me without that one.' With a heavy sigh, he added. 'I am usually very careful not to make assumptions about people, at least not on first acquaintance, but, since Caroline, I've tended to view beautiful women with a great deal of mistrust. No, that's not entirely true. Some beautiful women look knowing, are knowing, make it obvious; those I can cope with—their faces tell me what they're like. But Caroline, and you, looked so damned innocent, so unworldly, and that's dangerous!'

'I'm not dangerous,' she taunted softly.

'Much!' he snorted. 'I liked you, Neile,' he repeated after a few moments' silence, 'and then—well, when it all went wrong, I decided enough was enough. I'd devote the rest of my life to Daniel.'

'And then I followed you and mucked it all up again. I'm sorry. I do have this deplorable habit of acting first and thinking second.' Not entirely sure why she was apologising, or even what for, only knowing that she didn't want him to be hurt any more, she nuzzled her face into his shoulder. 'She has a lot to answer for, doesn't she? At least Gordon was honest, or stood by his own beliefs anyway.'

'Have you seen him since?' he asked with rather careful neutrality.

'No. Nor do I want to.'

'Yet you loved him once. . .'

'I thought I did,' she corrected, 'only now, of course, I know it was nothing of the sort.'

'Do you? How? How do you know, Neile?' he persisted.

Turning to look up at him, puzzled by the intensity in his voice, she asked in some bewilderment, 'How do I know it wasn't love?'

'Yes.'

'Because it wasn't like this, of course. How else would I know?'

Staring at her, his eyes searching hers, he finally asked slowly, 'Are you saying that you're in love with me? Or are you saying something else?'

Her body taut, she gave him back look for look. What did that mean? That he didn't want her to be in love with him? Or that he did? 'Are you playing games, Mackenzie?'

'No. No games. Answer the question. Please.'

'All right.' Looking away from him, hugging her arms round her knees, she confirmed quietly, 'Yes, I'm in love with you. Why else would I be here?'

'I don't know,' he admitted slowly.

Still not looking at him, she cleared her throat and asked carefully, 'And you? What do you feel?'

'Don't you know?'

'No.'

With an incredibly gentle hand, he turned her face towards him. 'Yes, you do. Oh, Neile,' he exclaimed on a sigh. 'I didn't expect this. To find that you wanted me, felt the same emotion I did, was a bonus I didn't dare look for when I made all these arrangements, and now— well, for once in my life I don't know what to say. Right now I'd even vanquish spiders for you.'

I don't want you to vanquish spiders, she thought with a little shiver of unhappiness. I want you to love me, and you don't, do you? You want me, which is an entirely different thing. Her beautiful eyes fixed on his, a haunting sadness in their depths, she gave him a tired smile. Feeling the warning prickle behind her eyes, knowing that at any moment she was going to cry, probably make a fool of herself, she scrambled quickly to her feet. 'Oh, my goodness, will you look at the time?' she exclaimed. 'Nearly three o'clock, and you still have to lock up.'

His face comically confused, he nodded. 'Yes, I'm sorry, Neile, I'm being very selfish. You must be exhausted.'

'Yes.' Desperately trying to hide her disappointment and hurt, she quickly pulled on her dress. Gathering up her scattered underwear, she made a hasty exit. She limped into her room, and quickly retrieved her night-dress and washing things from her case that had been left by the bed, and went into the bathroom. Quickly washing and cleaning her teeth, she pulled on her nightie. Just about to turn out the light, she heard voices and, thinking it might be Daniel calling, she edged the door open and peeped out. Mackenzie was leaning in through the door opposite, his voice reassuring as he talked with his son. He'd pulled on his trousers, but his torso gleamed nakedly, his feet bare.

'Did she come?' she heard Daniel ask sleepily, followed by Mackenzie's quiet affirmative. 'Is she staying?'

'Yes,' he admitted, and there was such a wealth of satisfaction in his voice that Neile frowned, puzzled by his fervency. 'Go back to sleep,' he continued, 'you'll see her in the morning.'

Quietly closing Daniel's door, he turned and saw Neile before she could duck back out of sight. With a warm smile, he walked across. 'Not fair, Neile, to wish me goodnight, then tempt me again.'

'I wasn't—didn't,' she mumbled hastily as she tried to close the door. 'I heard Daniel's voice and thought he might need something. . .'

'Not in case I might need something?' he teased, then frowned as he registered her withdrawal. 'What's wrong, Neile?'

'Nothing. I just didn't want you to think I was interfering, that's all.'

'Interfering?'

'In Daniel's welfare!'

'Why would I think you were interfering?' he asked in puzzlement. 'He's going to be your son, isn't he? Isn't he, Neile?' he asked urgently. 'Dear God, I know we didn't get around to discussing it, but——'

'My son?' she queried blankly.

'Well, of course your son! I thought you liked him!'

'I *do* like him!' she exclaimed in exasperation. 'What the hell's that got to do with anything?'

'Because life will be damned difficult if you don't!'

'Ssh!' she hissed. 'You'll wake him up again! Oh, for goodness' sake!' Grasping his arm, she dragged him into the room and closed the door. 'Now, explain in words of one syllable what you're talking about.'

'I don't know what I'm talking about! I don't know what the hell you're talking about! I merely wondered why you should think I should think you were interfering when as soon as it can be arranged you'll have every right to interfere with him! I think,' he added in obvious confusion. 'Hell, Neile, don't you want to marry me?'

'Marry you?' she squealed. 'Marry you?'

'Yes, marry me! Or are you trying to tell me you'll only marry me if I don't have Daniel?'

'Marry you?' she repeated. Her eyes wide and blank, she whispered hazily. 'You want to marry me?'

'Well, of course I want to marry you!' he exploded. Suddenly remembering Daniel, he lowered his voice theatrically. 'What in God's name did you think I wanted? A mistress?'

'Yes!' she said forcefully. 'What else was I supposed to think? You wouldn't answer when I asked you how you felt! Told me I knew, when I didn't know anything! You went on and on about mistrust. . .'

His face lightening, he dragged her into his arms. 'Damn you, Neile, what a wretched girl you are. I just think I've got it all sorted out and you confuse me all over again. Of course I want to marry you. I love you!'

'Well, how on earth was I supposed to know? You never said, not once!'

'Of course I did!'

'You did not! Not once!'

His eyes crinkled with humour, he laughed. 'Is that why you went off looking like a very crushed bluebell?'

'Bluebell?' she gurgled. 'I hope not. Snow White was bad enough.' Smiling up into his face, she slid her arms round his neck. Standing on tiptoe, she pressed her body against his. 'Are you really sure, Mackenzie? I mean, it's not that long since you were divorced—and we haven't known each other very long. . .'

'I'm sure,' he confirmed huskily. 'Sometimes you have to take chances, or you lose. And I don't want to lose, not any more. So, yes, I'm very, very sure.'

'OK. Well, if you're intending to make an honest woman of me, we don't need to say goodnight, do we?'

With a wicked grin, he swung her up into his arms. 'I was hoping you were going to say that.' When he'd laid her carefully on the bed, he picked up a book that was resting on the bedside table and handed it to her. 'Here,' he murmured with a teasing grin. 'I bought you a present.'

'When on earth did you have time to buy that?'

'On my way back from seeing Caroline.'

Pulling herself up on the pillows, she took it, then gave him an old-fashioned look as she saw what it was: *Your Future in the Stars*. Shaking her head at him, she opened it and riffled through it until she came to his star sign. Reading quickly through the character traits, she burst out laughing, 'Have you read this?'

'I glanced at it,' he informed her loftily.

'Liar, and you have to admit, Mackenzie, it's you to a "T". "Never a dull moment with this man. He can be passionate one minute, icy cold the next."' she read, then gave him a look of reproof when he snorted rudely. '"He has the planet Mars driving him, which gives him considerable business acumen and makes him bursting with ideas and creative energy." Oh, wow, I hope that bit's true. . .'

'Wicked girl, I thought you were supposed to be an innocent.'

'I am, but who said I'm not allowed to become— er. . .?'

'Debauched?' he asked hopefully.

'Debauched?' she exclaimed, laughing. 'Debauched?' Slapping his arm, she continued reading. '"He has a fiery heart. . ."'

'Oh, true, true. . .'

'Shut up. "His attitude to love is initially impulsive and he can lose interest easily"—you'd better not,' she told him severely.

Grinning, he taunted softly, 'It also says he likes to be the leader in a relationship. You have been warned, Miss Markham.'

'Huh.' Returning her wandering attention to the book, she finished reading the short passage. 'It also says that an Arien male is scrupulously faithful if he falls in love for keeps.' Raising her eyes to his, a hesitant query in their depths, she gave a shaky smile when he nodded, his own eyes gentle. 'Impatient, confident, generous.'

'Yes, that I think is true,' he agreed with wonderful conceit, 'which is more than can be said for your sign, let me add! Librans are supposed to be well balanced, mediators, calm and gentle!'

'I *am* calm and gentle. . .'

'Rubbish! At least I hope it's rubbish,' he whispered as he whisked the book out of her hands and tossed it on the floor, 'because I was hoping for a bit of wrestling round about now.' Standing, he quickly removed his trousers, whipped her nightie over her head and climbed into the bed. 'Don't forget, I have to be the leader.'

With a delighted giggle, she snuggled into his arms.

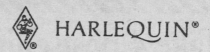 HARLEQUIN®

THE TAGGARTS OF TEXAS!

Harlequin's Ruth Jean Dale brings you
THE TAGGARTS OF TEXAS!

Those Taggart men—strong, sexy and hard to resist...

You've met Jesse James Taggart in FIREWORKS!
Harlequin Romance #3205 (July 1992)

And Trey Smith—he's THE RED-BLOODED YANKEE!
Harlequin Temptation #413 (October 1992)

Now meet Daniel Boone Taggart in SHOWDOWN!
Harlequin Romance #3242 (January 1993)

And finally the Taggarts who started it all—in LEGEND!
Harlequin Historical #168 (April 1993)

Read all the Taggart romances!
Meet all the Taggart men!

Available wherever Harlequin Books are sold.

Take 4 bestselling love stories FREE

Plus get a FREE surprise gift!

HARLEQUIN ROMANCE®

Some people have the spirit
of Christmas all year round...

People like Blake Connors
and Karin Palmer.

Meet them—and love them!—in
Eva Rutland's
ALWAYS CHRISTMAS.

Harlequin Romance #3240
Available in December wherever
Harlequin books are sold.

HRHX

WELCOME TO TYLER

The quintessential small town, where everyone knows everybody else!

Each book set in Tyler is a self-contained love story; together, the twelve novels stitch the fabric of the community.

"Scintillating romance!"
"Immensely appealing characters...wonderful intensity and humor."
Romantic Times

Join your friends in Tyler for the eleventh book, COURTHOUSE STEPS by Ginger Chambers, available in January.

Was Margaret's husband responsible for her murder? What memories come flooding back to Alyssa?

GREAT READING...GREAT SAVINGS...AND A FABULOUS FREE GIFT!

With Tyler you can receive a fabulous gift, ABSOLUTELY FREE, by collecting proofs-of-purchase found in each Tyler book. And use our special Tyler coupons to save on your next TYLER book purchase.

If you missed *Whirlwind* (March), *Bright Hopes* (April), *Wisconsin Wedding* (May), *Monkey Wrench* (June), *Blazing Star* (July), *Sunshine* (August), *Arrowpoint* (September), *Bachelor's Puzzle* (October), *Milky Way* (November) or *Crossroads* (December) and would like to order them, send your name, address, zip or postal code, along with a check or money order for $3.99 for each book ordered (please do not send cash), plus 75¢ postage and handling ($1.00 in Canada), payable to Harlequin Reader Service, to:

In the U.S.
3010 Walden Avenue
P.O. Box 1325
Buffalo, NY 14269-1325

In Canada
P.O. Box 609
Fort Erie, Ontario
L2A 5X3

Please specify book title(s) with your order.
Canadian residents add applicable federal and provincial taxes.

TYLER-11

HARLEQUIN PRESENTS®

A Year Down Under

Beginning in January 1993, some of Harlequin Presents's most exciting authors will join us as we celebrate the land down under by featuring one title per month set in Australia or New Zealand.

Intense, passionate romances, these stories will take you from the heart of the Australian outback to the wilds of New Zealand, from the sprawling cattle and sheep stations to the sophistication of cities like Sydney and Auckland.

Share the adventure—and the romance— of A Year Down Under!

Don't miss our first visit in **HEART OF THE OUTBACK** by Emma Darcy, Harlequin Presents #1519, available in January wherever Harlequin Books are sold. YDU-G

HARLEQUIN HISTORICAL CHRISTMAS STORIES · 1992 ·

Capture the magic and romance of Christmas in the 1800s with HARLEQUIN HISTORICAL CHRISTMAS STORIES 1992, a collection of three stories by celebrated historical authors. The perfect Christmas gift!

Don't miss these heartwarming stories, available in November wherever Harlequin books are sold:

MISS MONTRACHET REQUESTS by Maura Seger
CHRISTMAS BOUNTY by Erin Yorke
A PROMISE KEPT by Bronwyn Williams

Plus, as an added bonus, you can receive a FREE keepsake Christmas ornament. Just collect four proofs of purchase from any November or December 1992 Harlequin or Silhouette series novels, or from any Harlequin or Silhouette Christmas collection, and receive a beautiful dated brass Christmas candle ornament.

Mail this certificate along with four (4) proof-of-purchase coupons plus $1.50 postage and handling (check or money order—do not send cash), payable to Harlequin Books, to: **In the U.S.:** P.O. Box 9057, Buffalo, NY 14269-9057; **In Canada:** P.O. Box 622, Fort Erie, Ontario, L2A 5X3.

ONE PROOF OF PURCHASE

Name: _____

_____

Address: _____

_____

City: _____

State/Province: _____

Zip/Postal Code: _____

HX92POP   093 KAG